INN A BLUE MOON

Once

INN A BLUE MOON

LISA SAMSON

TATE PUBLISHING & *Enterprises*

Published by Tate Publishing & Enterprises, LLC
127 E. Trade Center Terrace | Mustang, Oklahoma 73064 USA
1.888.361.9473 | www.tatepublishing.com

Tate Publishing is committed to excellence in the publishing industry. The company reflects the philosophy established by the founders, based on Psalm 68:11,
"The Lord gave the word and great was the company of those who published it."

Book design copyright © 2011 by Tate Publishing, LLC. All rights reserved.
Cover design by Anna Lee
Interior design by Joel Uber

Published in the United States of America

ISBN: 978-1-61777-521-5
1. Fiction; Romance, Contemporary
2. Fiction;General
11.05.26

Dedication

This book is dedicated to Brian, Brianna, and Mom.
You enrich my life beyond words.

Acknowledgments

I would like to thank my husband, Brian. Without his sleepless nights the idea for this book would never have been born. His encouragement, unending enthusiasm, and support inspired me. My daughter, Brianna, for reminding me that a dream forgotten was never really a dream at all. And my mother, Betty, for her support and love through every season of my life. Thank you for your love and for being my first audience.

Prologue

Frank had made up his mind and was trying to explain to his friend, Rob, why he had to get away.

"I have to do something to get her voice out of my head!"

"Whose voice?"

"Carol's. I know it sounds crazy, but it is like I can hear her talking to me."

"And you think that spending a few days at a B and B in the desert is going to cure you?"

"The website said it was a place where your dreams could come true." Sheepishly he looked away, as he realized how ridiculous that sounded now.

"Sounds like you either need a shrink or a vacation, buddy. I hope you choose the right one."

Chapter One

Have you ever wondered what might have happened if…

You had not taken the wrong turn and ended up finding your dream house.

You hadn't gone on that blind date and met the love of your life.

You hadn't stayed at the Blue Moon Inn….

The wind swirled the dust and leaves around the yard, blowing dirt into the doorway as Gina pushed her way through with an armful of groceries. "Just great! Now I'm going to have to sweep that up after I put these away," she said to her cat, Oliver. Oliver raised his head and opened one eye, but easily went back to his cat napping. Not many things bothered Oliver. Living in the desert had a few drawbacks, and dust was one of them. She put the groceries on the counter and took out a broom and dustpan. Gina was meticulously clean, and it didn't go unnoticed by her guests. She had many customers who returned to the Blue Moon, and some she treated almost like family. It was an eclectic place, but everyone who stayed there had nothing but praise for it.

Gina had loved coming to the Blue Moon Inn when she was a kid to visit her aunt and uncle, who owned the place. She would help clean the rooms, wait on customers, and dream away as she gazed at the million stars at night. It was on Route 66, set back off the road, surrounded by beautiful cliffs. She always loved this place, but was surprised when her aunt and uncle asked her to move to New Mexico to run the Inn for them. They had no children of their own and wanted to travel and enjoy their "golden years," as her aunt had said. So, five years ago, she packed up everything she owned that would fit in her tiny car and headed east. She never looked back.

She disliked living in Los Angeles where she was born and raised. It just always seemed too busy and full of pollution. She felt like she could not take time to think or dream, that the city commanded all of her attention when she was there. Gina had always felt a connection with the Southwest desert and felt more peaceful when she was there. She had taken up yoga and grew most of her own vegetables. She also felt she had a gift for helping the guests at the Inn. She was very insightful and helped others see things in a different light. Even the Inn's website claimed that the Blue

Moon was an enchanted place where your dreams just might come true.

One of the surprises that awaited guests was the skylight in each room. They were clear so one could lie in bed and gaze at the stars all night. Stargazing was not just Gina's hobby; it was her passion. She hoped that it would be as enjoyable to those who stayed at the Blue Moon.

After putting away the groceries and sweeping up the dirt from the floor, Gina went to check in with Vivian to see if any of the guests had arrived. Vivian had worked at the Blue Moon for more than three years, and they seemed to make a good team. Vivian was a local and a hard worker. Gina had come to depend on her a great deal.

"Hi, Viv, any of the guests arrive yet?" Gina asked as she helped Vivian fold some towels.

"Only one so far. Mrs. West, or Kate, she said she prefers to be called. She seems very quiet and sad. I tried to interest her in some tea with me on the patio, but she said she just wanted to go to her room." Vivian put some more towels in the dryer.

"Thanks, Vivian. I'll check on her in a little while. She must have driven most of the day to get here; said she was coming from Phoenix. Maybe she just needs a little time away from the trials and humdrum of everyday life." Gina scooped up the bundle of towels.

"Maybe she is meeting another man!" exclaimed Vivian.

"Oh, you do have a devious mind!" Gina laughed.

"Well, why else would a married woman drive all the way here alone?" Vivian protested.

"If she were meeting another man, don't you think she would be a little more excited?"

"I guess so, but maybe that is just a cover up to throw us off the trail."

"You have been watching too many cop shows on TV. Now would you please take the rest of these towels for me, and stop making up stories about the guests." Gina chuckled as she left Vivian to her work.

In her room Kate West sat on the bed wondering what to do next. She had driven most of the day from Phoenix. She just needed to get away, clear her head, and decide what to do with the rest of her life. Somehow she thought that getting out of the city and in new surroundings would help. Matt told her to go. *Probably more out of pity than anything*, she told herself.

They had been married for five years and spent the last three trying to have a baby. She had become completely absorbed with conceiving a child, to the point that their marriage had almost dissolved. They had tried in vitro fertilization twice but could not afford to try it again. Matt did not want to adopt. He said if he couldn't have a child that was his, he didn't want to raise someone else's. He compared it to buying a used car. He would just be inheriting the other people's problems. He was a big believer in genetics, and no

LISA SAMSON

amount of pleading had changed his mind. How he could compare a child to a car was beyond her, but her therapist said it was just a man's way of trying to relate. Still, she thought it was cruel.

Kate was hoping that by stepping back from the situation, she could come to terms with living a life without children of her own. It seemed so unfair that women who didn't even want a baby had them, but the ones who desperately wanted one were unable to conceive. She knew that Matt was tired of hearing her talk and cry about it all the time. Their sex life had become a series of charts and temperatures, not the spontaneous love-making they used to enjoy. It felt more like work than pleasure, and Matt was expected to perform. She couldn't really blame him for distancing himself from her. She wondered if they would be able to salvage their marriage and move on.

She was feeling a little dizzy as she thought about it all, so she decided to lie down. Probably some residual side effects from the fertility drugs she had been taking a few weeks ago, she told herself. She had tried them in the past, and the only thing they seemed to do was make her irritable. Matt had told her that she could try them one more time, but if it didn't happen, then they were finished trying. He told her they needed to get back to some kind of normal life that didn't revolve around trying to make a baby 24/7. "Lots of couples don't have children and lead perfectly wonderful lives," he had said. Somehow, at this moment, she could not see how anything could be wonderful again. She rested her head on the pillow and gazed up at the skylight in the ceiling. She hoped it would not be so bright at night that it would keep her awake, not that she slept much these days anyway.

Just as Kate was dozing off, there was a tapping at the door. "Mrs. West, um, Kate, it's Gina from downstairs. I just wanted to see if there was anything I could get you to make your stay more comfortable."

A plus sign on the pregnancy test, Kate thought sarcastically. "No, thank you. I'm just going to rest before dinner." Kate exhaled as she laid her head back on the pillows.

"If you change your mind, I'll be downstairs." *Vivian is right. She does sound sad*, Gina thought.

The sun shone brilliantly through the small stained glass window at the end of the hall as Gina made her way back downstairs. The Blue Moon was not large, only ten rooms, but each one was decorated with a unique style. That was something Gina did once she began running the Inn. She also served dinner and breakfast to her guests, which was something that had been good for business. People liked the all-inclusive idea, and it helped Gina indulge her love of cooking. It also meant she did not have to eat alone, which she had come to dislike very much. As Gina turned to go down the steps, she got a funny feeling in the pit of her stomach. She smiled to herself. Whenever she had that feeling, it almost always meant something good was about to happen. She was excited to see what it would be this time.

As Gina reached the bottom of the stairs, she heard another guest coming in the front door. She rounded the corner in time to see a tall, nice looking man, trying his best to get a huge suitcase through the door. She watched him struggle with it for a minute, and finally he squeezed it through the door and put it on the floor. He looked up and a look of embarrassment crossed his face when he saw Gina. "I always over-pack," he said matter-of-factly.

"That's fine, we have plenty of room for your things. You must be Frank Webster," she said with a smile.

"Yes, I am." *He has a nice smile and kind eyes*, Gina thought. "Can I help you get your bag to your room?"

"No, no, I can manage it myself. I created this monster, and I will deal with it."

"Let me grab your room key, and I will show you to your room. How long will you be staying with us, Mr. Webster?" Gina asked as she went to her computer in the front hall.

"Please, call me Frank. I don't know exactly; do you need to have a definite day that I am leaving?" He frowned.

"No, not at all, stay as long as you would like."

She led the way up the stairs to the end of the hall and opened the door for Frank. He was still struggling to haul the huge suitcase up the stairs, but he finally made it to the top and rounded the corner. He was huffing and puffing and a piece of hair had fallen over one eye. He quickly pushed his hair back in place and entered the room that Gina had unlocked. "I hope this meets your approval," Gina said stepping aside for him.

"It is fine, just fine," replied Frank as he gave the suitcase one more heave into the room.

"If there is anything you need, please let me know. And remember, dinner is served at six," Gina said with a smile.

"Thank you," Frank answered as he shoved the suitcase to one side of the room.

Gina slipped quietly out the door. She already thought he was a very interesting person, but she had the feeling he didn't know that about himself yet.

Frank scolded himself for packing so much stuff. Carol always made fun of him for over-packing when they were married. She said nobody else needed to pack anything, because he brought enough for everyone. He said that one never knew when one might need something, so he always tried to be prepared. He liked the feeling of being organized. But maybe that is what drove Carol away. She complained that he never did anything spontaneously, that every minute had to be planned. Their lives had become boring and predictable she said, but what did she expect after fifteen years?

No amount of organizing had made him feel any better after Carol moved out. He had gotten rid of some of the furniture and bought some new things. What he didn't replace he rearranged, but it still did not fill the terrible void inside. He had come to the Blue Moon to make a new plan, but, as of yet, he didn't know what that was exactly. He was hoping to be inspired by the desert, but so far he felt hot and dusty, not inspired in the least. He decided to unpack and then freshen up before dinner. He wondered again what had possessed him to come here, but here he was, so he was going to try and make the best of it. Maybe it was the promise on the website that it was an enchanted place where your dreams just might come true. If nothing else, it was nice to get away, he decided.

He promised himself he was not going to spend every waking minute thinking of Carol and what she might be doing at that exact moment. He had heard from a mutual friend that she was seeing someone, and he wondered what he was like. *Is he good looking, younger, more spontaneous, or all of those things?* His pride wouldn't allow him to ask his friend or Carol.

He was so lonely that sometimes he felt as if he would go crazy. His friends kept trying to get him to go out with other women, and he did once. It was a blind date, and the woman kept talking about her former husband and how he was a no-good cheat. She was angry at men in general, because her husband had an affair. When she wasn't talking about him, she was talking about her dog, Dixie, and all the things she could do. He hardly got to say anything during the entire evening and decided right then that he was done with blind dates. It had been eight months since the divorce was final, and he knew it was time to start a new chapter. The trouble was he didn't know where to begin.

He had considered changing careers, but he lacked the confidence to leave the company he had worked for since he got out of college. His job was not excit-ing to most people, but Frank still enjoyed it most of the time. He liked working with numbers. It was easier than working with people. It was either right or wrong, black or white, no gray areas. He knew where he stood with numbers, and there was no guessing. He had a nice office with a window, and it was a short commute for him.

That was part of the reason Carol let him have the house, as her job was on the other side of town, and she wanted a shorter commute. Maybe it would have been easier if they had sold the house and both got-ten a different place to live. Sometimes the memories they had made in the house made him even sadder. He had known for some time that things weren't great between them, but he figured it was just because they had been married for so long. They didn't really argue much. It was more Carol putting him down or telling him what he was doing wrong. Carol always seemed to get her way in the end, as she was very stubborn.

Frank was sorry that he hadn't been able to convince her that they should have a child. She was adamant that it just wasn't the right time. First, it was because she was trying to get established in her career. Then it was she was working too much, and it wouldn't be fair to a child to have an absent mother. Then it was that Frank wouldn't be enough help to her, and they couldn't afford a nanny. Finally, Frank just stopped asking. He always wondered in the back of his mind if Carol would have had a child if she had been married to someone else. He guessed it was for the best now, because the divorce would have been hard on a child and maybe harder on him as well. Although he had a hard time imagining how it could be much harder than it already was.

When Frank had met Carol, he thought she was the most exciting woman he had ever met. She was giving a speech at their college on women's rights, and he thought she was beautiful. It took all the courage he could muster to just say hello to her afterward. He saw her again at a party on campus a couple of weeks later and decided to talk to her. He had been drinking a little and had more courage than usual. He was surprised that she remembered him, and they talked the rest of the evening. He invited her to a movie the next week, and she accepted. After that, they began seeing each other every day.

Frank felt like he had won the lottery. Carol was smart, witty, and beautiful. He was amazed that she wanted him. Maybe that was where he made his first mistake in their relationship. He was so eager to please her that he agreed to whatever she wanted. They ate where she wanted to eat, saw only the movies she chose, and even hung out with only her friends. Frank pretty much stopped hanging out with his guy friends as his world became so narrow that it eventually was snubbed out by Carol's. By the time they were married, Carol had stopped asking Frank for his opinion about anything. He had put his foot down about one thing though, and that was the house. He had found it and knew that it would be a good investment for them. She had wanted something more modern, so he compromised by letting her decorate the house if she would agree to buy it. He guessed he should have negotiated that a little better, because her idea of decorating had cost him dearly. Maybe that was another reason she let him have the house; she had never really liked it from the start.

LISA SAMSON

Chapter Two

Maggie sped along the curvy road with the top of her convertible down, relishing the feeling of the wind blowing in her hair. She felt daring for the first time in a long time. She felt alive. She had decided on a whim to take a road trip and see where she ended up for the night. She was a writer and was having a bad case of writers' block. She was hoping that getting away would be what she needed to get the juices flowing again.

Maggie had felt blocked in most areas of her life for quite some time, if she told herself the truth. Nothing had been the same after Neal died. Life wasn't fair, she had decided, but what else could she do but go on? Neal had begged her not to mourn too long and to try and find love and happiness. *He knew me so well*, she thought now. He knew she was too vivacious to sit in the house wearing black and sealing herself off from the world.

The cancer had taken a toll on Neal's body, but it never affected his spirit. When he was first diagnosed, he decided that whatever time he had left would be spent to the fullest. He refused to feel sorry for himself and accepted no pity. Instead, he and Maggie traveled to Europe, spent evenings on the deck enjoying a margarita, and reminisced about all the wonderful things they had shared. Seventeen years was not long enough to be with a man like Neal, but she was grateful for the time they had and for their daughter, Elizabeth. She was busy with her first year of college, which was a blessing because she had adored her father. She took it very hard when he was diagnosed with cancer, and Maggie had tried her best to put on a brave front for her sake. But Elizabeth knew instinctively that her father was not going to win the battle and immediately began researching all of his possible options for treatment. Neal did the treatment his doctor recommended but drew the line at the experimental things Elizabeth wanted him to try. He said he would rather spend that time with his family, and that is exactly what he did.

Maggie rounded another corner and was jolted back to reality. She was getting tired and hungry and began looking for a place to stop for the night. Up ahead she saw a sign for the Blue Moon Inn; meals included, it said. She decided that it would be an interesting place to stop, and she wouldn't have to leave for dinner. She hoped they still had rooms available. Maggie was not much of a planner, but rather preferred to live in the moment and be spontaneous. It had made for an interesting life, although not always the easiest.

She slowed the car, took the next exit, and headed for the Blue Moon. As she pulled up in front of the two-story building, she didn't see too many cars in the lot, so she breathed a sigh of relief. The Inn was painted in earth tones and was made of stucco. It had huge wooden beams extending out from the roof line, giving it a very Southwestern feel. There were red flowers in large pots lining the flagstone walkway, and a brightly colored blanket draped over a chair near the door. Maggie thought it looked charming and decided to head inside. Gina looked up as she came in. "Welcome to the Blue Moon. Will you be staying with us?"

"Yes, at least, if you have a room available," stammered Maggie, "I didn't have a reservation." Maggie was trying to smooth down her windblown hair with one hand.

"How long will you be staying with us?" Gina asked, as she grabbed a key from the counter.

"Oh, just one night, maybe two." Suddenly, Maggie was unsure what her plans were, but thought she probably wouldn't stay longer than that.

"Then I have the perfect room for you." Gina led the way up the stairs and opened the door half way down the hall. Maggie followed her into the room and set her small suitcase down. She caught a glimpse of herself in the mirror and broke out in laughter.

"I have been driving most of the day with the top down on my convertible," she explained. "I guess I didn't bother combing my hair before getting out of the car." Maggie tried unsuccessfully to smooth her wild hair into submission.

"Looks just fine," Gina said, as she handed Maggie the key. "Dinner is at six sharp; see you downstairs."

And with that Gina closed the door behind her, leaving Maggie to wonder what to do until dinner. She took some time to look around the room and smiled to herself when she saw the skylight in the ceiling. Neal had always loved stargazing, and they had spent many nights lying outside on a blanket just looking at the stars and enjoying the closeness. Her heart ached with fresh grief as she thought about it. Shaking her head as if to clear the memories away, she decided to try and do something with her hair.

Gina hurried into the kitchen to finish the dinner preparations. She always made extra food, just in case someone checked-in unexpectedly. She was meticulous when it came to feeding her guests, and it was something she truly enjoyed. She checked the chicken in the oven before heading to the refrigerator to take out the salad ingredients. She was chopping peppers and carrots when Vivian came in to see if she needed any help.

"Smells wonderful." Vivian reached over and grabbed a carrot off the counter.

"You can go out and make sure the table is set and put the water pitcher on the table if you don't mind." Gina finished chopping the vegetables for the salad. Vivian left the kitchen to check on the dining room.

She enjoyed working for Gina, and was glad that she made her feel more like family than an employee.

In his room, Frank was debating how to dress for dinner. He had put a tie on but decided that would be too formal. He didn't want to wear jeans, as that might be too informal. No wonder he packed so many clothes; he could never seem to make the simplest decisions. *Maybe it is because you give yourself too many options,* he heard Carol's voice in his head. Surely that voice, her voice, would eventually go away, wouldn't it? He sincerely hoped so because he was getting tired of listening to it. Finally he decided on khaki pants and a blue polo shirt. He checked himself in the mirror one last time, making sure his hair was in place before leaving the room. He could already smell something delicious as he stepped into the hallway. ·

When he arrived in the dining room another lady was already seated. "Hi, I'm Frank." He smiled as he extended his hand.

"I'm Kate," the woman replied but did not look him in the eye.

He thought she must have something to hide or was terribly sad; he couldn't decide which. She was a petite woman, that appeared to be close to thirty and her shoulders sagged as if she was carrying the weight of the world. He took a seat across the table from her. Just then, he noticed another woman coming into the dining room. She looked to be close to his age and had a mop of curls piled on top of her head. When she saw him, she smiled, and somehow it lit up her whole face.

"Hi, I'm Maggie," she said.

"I'm Frank, and this is Kate." Frank stood and reached to shake her hand. Kate lifted her gaze briefly and mumbled a hello. Maggie already thought that she was not going to enjoy this woman's company. Maggie took a seat next to Frank, because at least he seemed friendly. Gina and Vivian began bringing in bowls of food, and after the guests were served, both sat down to join them. Everyone began to eat and comment on how delicious the food was. Gina explained that she grew all of the vegetables herself.

"I used to like to garden," Kate said unexpectedly. She had been very quiet through most of dinner.

"Why don't you garden anymore?" Gina asked, hoping she would open up a little. "I...I...don't know," she stammered.

How could she tell these complete strangers that the last few years she had been too preoccupied with trying to conceive a child? She had forgotten that she used to really enjoy gardening. Well, maybe this was a sign that she needed to get on with her life, she decided. For the first time all evening, she smiled. "I think I'll take it up again." She picked up her fork and finished her salad.

Frank was entertained with Maggie's stories of her many travels and adventures. She seemed so confident and sure of herself. All of them enjoyed Maggie's tales. She had a way of making them seem humorous. Frank had always wanted to be that person at dinner parties.

But somehow he seemed to struggle to make small talk, always wondering if he was too boring.

After dinner and dessert everyone seemed more relaxed. Frank and Maggie had been chatting almost nonstop, and even Kate seemed to be in a little lighter mood. Gina and Vivian cleared the table and began taking things into the kitchen. They could hear Frank and Maggie on the front porch having a lively discussion about their travels. Apparently, Frank used to travel some for business, and they had been to some of the same places.

Kate was sitting in the living area looking at the books on the shelves.

"She seems really sad about something, doesn't she?" Gina began putting dishes in the dishwasher.

"Who, Kate?" replied Vivian. "Sad and lost. It makes you wonder what tragedy has happened in her life." Vivian handed Gina the last of the plates.

"Well the other two seem to be hitting it off." Gina smiled. "There is always some magic at the Blue Moon."

Chapter Three

Damian stood staring at the baggage carousel waiting for his luggage to come off the plane. It had been a very long flight back from overseas. He had tried to sleep and couldn't. He tried to watch some movies, but his mind kept wandering. His world had been turned upside down since his mother passed away three months ago. They had let him come home for the funeral, but then he had to go back to the Middle East. In a way it had been a blessing, because he was so busy fighting the war on terrorism that he didn't have much time to think about everything that had happened. At least not until now.

He was twenty-seven years old and had practically no family left. His father had died ten years ago, but at least that was expected. His father was much older than his mother and had not been in the best of health. But when Damian got word that his mother had been killed in a car accident, he just somehow couldn't believe it. Even at the funeral it seemed surreal. Due to the extent of her injuries, he had decided not to have an open casket at the service. He always felt it was harder to say good-bye to someone if you couldn't see them, but he knew his mother would not have wanted anyone to see her in that condition.

He had two aunts and two uncles and a handful of cousins, but other than that the only family he had was the Corps. He was closer to some of the men he served with than he had been to most people in his life. He had become especially fond of one of his commanding officers who had helped him tremendously with the grief he was feeling over the past few months. Colonel Alexander had taken Damian under his wing. Damian had been assigned to his staff right after they arrived and enjoyed working for the colonel. He was an honest man and had been in the Corps since before Damian was born. The colonel had a loyalty and integrity about him that was rare, and he respected him immensely. He sincerely hoped that he would get the opportunity to serve with Colonel Alexander again.

Now he was on leave for the next thirty days and then was to report to his stateside duty at Camp Pendleton in California. He was going home to Colorado to tie up the loose ends of his mother's estate, and then he was going to drive to California. He was not at all sure he was ready to do this. It would be very difficult to go through all of her things. It had been his mother's wish for the house, and anything Damian didn't want, to be sold so he could use the money to buy a home of his own one day. She knew him well. He always had a heart for travel and was very duty-driven. It was her worst fear and yet her proudest moment when he graduated from boot camp. He loved the Marine Corps, and she knew that he was doing what made him happy. She had chided him about settling down and giving her grandchildren, but she never pushed too hard. Now he felt a pang of guilt that he hadn't settled down and given her the pleasure of at least one grandchild. He wasn't opposed to it, but he just hadn't found the right woman.

Damian found his bags and headed outside. Greg, his friend since grade school, was picking him up and taking him home. *Home has a funny sound to it*, he thought. It would just never feel like it was home again without his mom there. He wondered if he would ever feel at home anywhere again. It was a brilliantly sunny day, and Damian squinted into the rays to try and see if Greg was anywhere in sight. He finally spotted him inching his way in traffic in the old blue Ford. Greg was sure one day it would be a classic, but Damian was just as certain that it would not. He smiled as he waved to his friend.

"There's the hard-charger!" Greg was grinning from ear to ear as Damian swung the door closed. Damian reached over and patted Greg on the back.

"Thanks for picking me up; I really appreciate it," Damian said.

"What are friends for?" Greg smiled as he inched his way along in traffic. "Are you hungry? Because if you are, I know a great little place to grab a bite, and it's on our way."

"I am starving! I didn't eat much food on the plane, so I'm famished," Damian replied.

They drove to a little café near the downtown area. It had a coffee cup with a drop of coffee spilling out lit up in the front. They found a table near the back and proceeded to look at the menu. "When you're hungry everything looks good." Damian scanned the menu trying to make up his mind.

"They have great burgers here, and the wings are good too," Greg offered.

After the waitress came and took their order, Greg sat back and took a long look at his friend. His eyes were weary, and there were dark circles under them. The lines on his face showed he was troubled and his eyes held sadness deep within them. Damian had never been one to share his problems. He always felt he should not burden others, but rather deal with things on his own. This had served him well in the Corps, but in personal matters, it sometimes proved to be difficult.

After lunch Greg drove Damian home. "You want me to come in?" Greg asked as he pulled the car to a stop.

"No, I've got to face the ghosts sometime, and I guess this is as good as any."

He was tired to the bone. *Maybe it's jet lag,* he thought. Maybe it was that he had not dealt with his mother's unexpected death, and now it was being forced upon him.

Damian let himself into the house and set his duffle bag down in the hallway. It was eerily quiet. There were no happy greetings, no smell of food cooking in the kitchen. He realized that he was utterly and completely alone. He wandered through the house, touching things absentmindedly. Everything looked as if someone still lived there, except for some dust accumulating on the furniture. He sat down on the couch and suddenly realized he was crying. He buried his face in his hands and sobbed for the first time since his mother died. He felt like an orphan, even though he was twenty-seven years old.

He didn't know what to do next. He decided he was too tired to make rational decisions, so he took a long, hot shower. As the water ran over him, he started to relax a little. After that he went to his old room and lay on the bed. The next thing he knew, he was awoken by the sun streaming in through the window. He looked at the clock and realized he had been asleep for nearly fourteen hours.

He got up and made his way to the kitchen. He wondered if any of the food in the house was still edible. He found some cereal bars and a Coke in the refrigerator and decided to call it breakfast. He had eaten much worse in his years in the Corps, like snails in the jungle. He turned the thermostat up to take the chill out of the air. He was grateful his mom had put all of the utilities on automatic payments from her account, so he didn't have to worry about that, at least for now. His mom had left him a sizeable life insurance policy, some savings, and of course the house. He had put most of the money in a savings account until he could decide what to do next. No amount of money would persuade him to leave the Marine Corps, but at least it would be there for him in the future if he needed it. Damian thought he might want to get married one day, but he knew what a sacrifice that would be for a woman to live the life the Corps demanded. He had dated many women, but none he could see himself settling down and having a family with.

He began to ramble through the house, wondering what to do with himself. Everything now belonged to him, and he didn't know where to start. He had hired a cleaning service to clean twice a month and check on things while he decided what to do next. He wasn't quite ready to sell the house. It was paid for now, so it was not a huge expense to keep it. It was the place where he grew up and spent most of his life. He just couldn't part with it yet, although he couldn't really see himself settling down here either.

He looked at the letter Colonel Alexander had given him before he returned to the States. It was a letter from his mom that the attorney had mailed to his unit to be given to him. Somehow he had not been able to bring himself to open it. He had been so focused on fighting terrorists that he had shut down his emotions about everything else. At least that is the way it was until now. He felt emotionally spent after his crying jag from the night before. He tried to tell himself it was because he was tired and jet lagged, but he knew deep down it was from pure grief.

He plopped down on the couch and turned on the television. Flipping through channels mindlessly, he couldn't concentrate on anything long enough to watch it. He had never felt so alone and overwhelmed in his life. He had four weeks before he was to report back to the Marine Corps; he couldn't imagine what he was going to do with all that time. He felt like he needed to do something, but, for the life of him, he didn't know what it was. He decided to go for a walk, hoping that would clear his mind. He grabbed his jacket and the house key and headed out the door. He couldn't decide which way to walk but finally headed toward the downtown area.

He stopped and bought a hot dog at a stand on the corner and decided that would be lunch. He kept moving, not really seeing much of anything around him. His walk had turned into a run. If he ran long enough, maybe he could escape this feeling inside of him. He had been running for over thirty minutes when it began to rain. At first only a few drops were irritating him as he kept running. But with every step the rain became heavier, matching the feeling in his heart. Being a Marine had prepared him for persevering in any weather, so he continued to run. An hour later he was back at the house, looking like a drowned rat. There was not one inch of him that didn't drip water, yet somehow he felt numb to it all.

He let himself in and stripped off the wet clothes. After a hot shower, he decided to try and take a nap. Surely after some rest this feeling would go away. He lay on his bed and tried to sleep. Instead he found himself staring up at the ceiling. He knew what he had to do. He had to get away from this house. He just couldn't deal with it, not now and maybe not ever. He was alone in the world, and he felt foolish for feeling like an orphan. After all, he had the Marine Corps and that was his family now. He grabbed the keys to his mom's car, still parked in the garage. He packed a change of clothes and, at the last minute, took the letter from the attorney he had yet to read. He headed out the door and down the highway, destination unknown.

Chapter Four

Kate decided to take a walk behind the Inn after dinner. There was a small garden with a fountain and beautiful flowers. If made her feel very tranquil. The flowers were brilliant shades of purple and yellow, and the fountain filled the air with soothing sounds. She thought about calling Matt, but somehow she really didn't want to talk to him. She knew she was still angry with him because he refused to adopt or keep trying to have a baby. She also knew that if her marriage was going to survive she was going to have to forgive him and move forward.

Kate sat down on a glider facing the garden and began to glide back and forth in an easy rhythm. She realized that she had been so focused on trying to have a baby that she had not given any thought to what her life could be like without one. It still seemed almost incomprehensible to her, but she was beginning to look at the possibilities at least. Maybe talking to the therapist had helped more than she thought. Looking ahead was progress, no matter how you looked at it. She decided when she got home, she was going to get out her gardening tools and plant some new roses along the fence. It was the first time in a long time that she had made a decision about something other than work and fertility schedules, and it felt good.

As she glided back and forth, a wave of nausea swept over her. She hoped it wasn't something she ate for dinner, because she really didn't want to be in an Inn full of people who all had food poisoning at the same time. She sat still for a few minutes and the nausea subsided. Maybe it was the leftover effects of the fertility drugs, but she didn't remember feeling this way the last time she had taken them. Just then Oliver, the cat, jumped up beside her and rubbed his head on her arm. She stroked his fur as he purred loudly. *Maybe I should get a cat*, she thought. It wouldn't replace a baby, but at least it was something she could love and care for. Kate could hear Frank and Maggie talking in the front driveway, but couldn't quite make out what they were saying. She decided to just sit and be quiet. She wasn't unsociable, she just didn't feel like talking to anyone at the moment.

Frank was looking at Maggie's convertible and telling her how unsafe he had always thought them to be. Maggie laughed and tossed her unruly hair over her shoulder.

"You can't live your life afraid of everything, Frank. Come for a ride with me, and you will understand why it is worth the risk."

Maggie was already headed toward the driver's side of the car. Frank hesitated for a moment. He could hear Carol's voice again nagging him about always playing it safe.

"I'm up for a ride if you are!"

Maggie hopped over the door and into the seat, as Frank swung the passengers' door open and got in. He immediately fastened his seatbelt. Maggie took one look at him and laughed as the engine roared to life, and she took off into the dust.

"Hang on!" she shouted.

Maggie drove over hills and around the corners of the road that had led her to the Blue Moon. The wind rushed through her hair, and she had a huge grin on her face as Frank looked over at her. He had to remind himself to stop looking at her and tried to focus on the scenery around them. Red rocks jutted out over canyons with yellow and gold light playing in the shadows as the sun got lower in the sky. He couldn't decide which was more beautiful, the scenery or the driver. He felt like a school boy again as he watched Maggie expertly shift through the gears and whiz around the corners. The wind made his eyes water a little, but he was determined not to think about what could happen if they crashed and the car rolled over. Instead he focused on Maggie. She was everything he was not. She was outgoing, impulsive, unafraid…alive. Maggie slowed the car at the next corner and pulled off at a scenic overlook. The view was breathtaking. She could imagine cowboys moving across the desert on their horses, and cattle grazing for miles and miles. *Maybe I'll use that in my next story,* she thought.

"What did you think?" Maggie turned to look at Frank.

"It was… exhilarating," he stammered.

"You can turn loose of the door now," Maggie teased.

Frank looked down at the death grip he had on the door, and released to his chagrin. Frank got out of the car and walked over to the guardrail at the edge of the overlook while Maggie followed. The rocks came out to a small point beneath them before they turned jagged and steep. A roadrunner ran past them as they stood admiring the view. The sun was beginning to set, and the sky was etched with pink and blue hues.

"Do you always drive with the top down?" Frank asked.

"If it is above sixty degrees, I do. Even if I have to wear a jacket, the feeling I get is worth it." Maggie moved closer to the edge, taking in the view.

"Is this your first time to ride in a convertible, Frank?" Maggie looked over at him.

"Yes," he said to his chagrin. "It was always one of those things I wanted to do one day but just never got around to it." Frank was a little embarrassed to tell her the truth, but he was an honest man.

"Well, you can mark that one off of the list then." She smiled as she walked back and hopped in the car.

They were quiet on the drive back to the Inn, each with their own thoughts. Frank wondered what Carol would say if she had seen him ride in a convertible. *Why do I even care*, he wondered? He had lived so many years worrying about what Carol thought about everything, he suddenly realized that he didn't have to think about that anymore. He could do what he wanted when he wanted. He kept trying to make that nagging voice in his head go away. He decided he had to make it stop, or it was going to make him crazy.

Maggie was deep in thought about Neal. Having another man in the car with her felt like she was betraying him somehow. She knew that he had hoped she would find love again and didn't want her to be alone. She was too much of a people person to live a solitary life. *Maybe it is too soon*, she thought. But it had been fourteen months; she had to start living again. She was able to sleep through the night finally, and there were stretches of time when she didn't think about him. But in some way she felt guilty for that too. She would lie in bed at night and imagine what it felt like to have his arms around her. As time passed it became harder for her to imagine, and she struggled to hold on to the memory.

She pulled back into the parking lot at the Inn, and she and Frank got out of the car.

"Thank you." He smiled at her. His hair was wild, all over the place, and hanging over one eye. Maggie suddenly began to laugh out loud.

"What's so funny?" Frank asked.

"Look at your hair!"

Frank leaned over and looked in the side mirror of the car. He quickly tried to push his hair back in place. Maggie decided to check her hair too and laughed even harder at her reflection in the mirror. She pulled a brush out of her purse and ran it through her wavy hair, then handed it to Frank. He smoothed his hair back into place. They stood there looking at each other and laughing out loud. Maggie had the bluest eyes, and they had crinkles in the corners when she laughed. *She must laugh a lot*, Frank thought.

They walked around to the side of the Inn and sat down in the big gazebo. Gina had put some lemonade and cookies out there earlier, and Frank helped himself to both.

"You are the only woman I know that can drive a stick shift." He hoped that sounded like the compliment he had intended it to be.

"I grew up on a farm, so I had to learn out of necessity." Maggie looked out across the desert. Frank asked her about where she had grown up and her family and Maggie entertained him with stories of her youth.

He wished he had such fond memories of his childhood. Instead they mostly consisted of his mother hovering over him, worried that he would have another asthma attack. He had been an only child, born to his parents later in life, and they were overprotective, to say the least. They had been gone now for nearly seven years, but sometimes he still missed them. He knew his mother would have been very disappointed that he and

Carol divorced. She had adored Carol and thought she was the best thing that could have happened to him. Frank had thought so, too, for a while. But in many ways she had treated him like a child and had become very condescending and bitter. Still, it was hard to be all alone sometimes.

It was getting dark and there was a chill in the air.

"I guess I better go up to my room and try to get some rest," Maggie stood as she said it. "I hope I can sleep with that huge skylight over the bed," Maggie admitted as she walked along the rock pathway.

"Well, if you can't, at least you have something to look at besides the ceiling. But I know what you mean. I wondered the same thing when I saw the skylight over my bed."

Frank followed Maggie up the steps into the Inn. It had been the best evening Frank had in a long time, and he was sorry to see it end. As they got to the lobby they said good night and went their separate ways to their rooms. Frank knew he would be thinking about those blue eyes as he drifted off to sleep.

Chapter Five

Damian was driving but had no destination in mind. He was driving his mom's car that had been in the garage. She had only used it if she was driving long distances. Otherwise, she drove an old mini-van. She said she liked having all that room. That is what she was driving when she was hit by a guy who was high on meth. He was in jail still awaiting trial, but the district attorney assured Damian he would push for the maximum sentence. But no matter how long the sentence, it wasn't going to bring his mother back.

He stopped at a drive thru to get some food and kept on driving. The radio was on, but Damien was not really listening. He was hoping it would help drown out the helplessness he felt, but so far it wasn't working. Even after driving all night, he was afraid to try and sleep. Weary to the bone, but not sleepy. Wondering again for the thousandth time what went through his mom's mind right before she died. *Did she know she was dying? Was she afraid? Did she think of him? Was she in a horrible amount of pain?* These were questions that would remain unanswered in this lifetime.

Thinking of his mom suffering was an image he could hardly bear. She had always been a sweet and loving person, not one who deserved to spend her last minutes suffering. He thought back over the years and all the things his mom had done for him. The birthday party when he was eight, with a real live pony for the kids to ride. He had been the envy of all of his friends that day. The occasional twenty dollars she would tuck in his sock drawer, so he would think he had put it there and just forgotten about it. The wonderful vacations they shared going to Disney World and the beach. Skiing in the mountains and the way she made hot chocolate when they were finished for the day. He didn't realize that tears were streaming down his face again, nor did he even bother wiping them away; he just kept driving.

As the sun was coming up, he noticed some beautiful red cliffs in the distance. The light danced on the crevices, giving it the appearance of being alive. He could not help but smile to himself. He remembered that he had crossed the border into New Mexico, but he wasn't really sure what town he was near. After looking at the gas gauge he decided he better stop at the next station.

He pulled into the station and began pumping gas. An elderly man struck up a conversation as he emptied the trash cans. Damian could barely see his eyes because his face was so wrinkled and tan.

"Not from around here, are ya, son? Noticed the Colorado plates." The man stooped as he picked up an empty bottle off the ground.

"No, sir, I'm just passing through," Damian replied.

"Been driving all night?" he asked as he continued to empty the trash.

Damian thought he must look a little disheveled; he had been in the same clothes for nearly twenty-four hours.

"Yes sir." Damian didn't want to be rude, but he didn't feel much like talking.

"Well then, you should take the next exit down the highway and stop at the Blue Moon Inn. It is the last place to stay for more than a hundred miles. Nice place, not too pricey. Tell Gina I sent you, and she'll take good care of you." He tied the trash bag and sat it on the ground.

"Thank you. I might just do that." Suddenly a warm bed sounded awfully good to Damian. He was tired to the bone. He pulled his jacket around him and climbed back in the car. He decided that he was too tired to keep driving, and he couldn't think straight anymore. He pulled back onto the highway and headed for the next exit. Damian pulled up to the Blue Moon Inn and turned off the engine. It was very quiet, but it was very early in the morning he reminded himself. There were lights on inside, so he took that as a good sign that someone was up. He grabbed his bag and headed inside. Oliver spotted him and began making circles around his feet as he made his way to the desk. "Good Morning!" Gina greeted him as he came in the door. She had seen him pull up in the driveway. Damian noticed a wonderful smell in the air, a mixture of bacon and maple syrup.

"I was wondering if you have a room. I've been driving all night, and the man at the gas station suggested I stop here," Damian said. Gina could see the dark circles under his eyes.

"That would be Rex. Yes, we have a room. Do you know how long you plan to stay?" Gina said as she looked at him. His shoulders sagged, and he looked a little lost.

"Only one day, maybe tonight also, then I'll be on my way," Damian said and handed her his credit card. Gina handed him the key and asked if he would like to have breakfast before going upstairs.

"It is included in the room fee, so you might as well eat." Gina gestured toward the kitchen.

"It smells delicious; don't mind if I do."

Damian smiled and sat down at the long wooden table, and Gina brought out a plate full of pancakes and bacon. She had fresh fruit, coffee, and juice too. Damian ate every bite. He hadn't realized just how hungry he was until he smelled the food cooking. It was the closest thing to a home cooked meal he had eaten in months. He finished the last of his juice and headed up to his room.

LISA SAMSON

The room was decorated in blues and greens, and was very clean. It had an antique table beside the bed and some Southwestern art framed on the walls. The quilt on the bed was blue, green, and beige and made of durable material and went well with the decor. Damian showered quickly and brushed his teeth before falling into bed. He fell asleep so fast that he didn't even notice the skylight above his bed. In his mind he was already dreaming of his mom and the happy times they shared.

As the sun grew higher in the sky, one by one the other guests came downstairs for breakfast. Maggie had taken a little extra time with her hair, and Frank had changed clothes three times before finally settling on something to wear. He felt silly for caring, but at the same time he felt more alive and invigorated than he had in a long time. Frank made a point to sit across from Maggie, so he could look at her beautiful blue eyes.

The smell of pancakes and bacon wafted through the first floor of the Inn, and fresh coffee was in ample supply. Kate came down a little later and asked if she could just have some coffee.

"Are you sure you're not hungry?" Gina asked.

"I'm not feeling the best, but maybe I will feel better after some coffee."

Gina thought she looked a little pale but said nothing. Frank and Maggie were so engrossed in conversation that they didn't notice Kate take her cup of coffee and head out to the patio. Gina made a mental note to check on Kate later. After breakfast, Maggie asked Gina if it would be possible for her to stay another night at the Inn. She said she felt inspired to do some writing since she arrived and didn't want to lose her motivation. Gina wondered if Frank had inspired her somehow, as the two of them seemed to hit it off. Frank asked Maggie if she would like to go into town for some lunch and a look around, and Maggie agreed. She wanted to do some writing, but said she would be ready for a break by noon.

Gina cleared the last of the breakfast dishes and began loading them in the dishwasher. Oliver was circling her feet, meaning he was waiting to be fed. "Just a minute my little man. Let me put the dishes in here first, and then I will get you some food."

Gina was on her own until later in the afternoon when Vivian would be back to work at the Inn. She had asked Gina if she could have the morning off because she needed to take her grandmother to a doctor's appointment. Gina didn't mind, she could manage for a little while on her own, and Vivian rarely asked for time off.

Vivian's family had made Gina feel like part of the clan, inviting her over for holidays and impromptu dinners when things were slow at the Inn. They were a large and interesting group, native to the area, and Gina loved to listen to their stories. She finished loading the dishwasher and went to the cupboard to get

Oliver some food. All of a sudden she heard a thump out on the back patio. She rushed out to find Kate out cold, lying on the ground. Gina quickly checked for a pulse and breathing and was relieved to find both.

"Kate! Kate! Can you hear me, Kate?" Gina shouted. Kate's eyelids fluttered a little, and then she opened her eyes. Her face was pale as a ghost.

"I think I must have fainted." Kate tried to smile.

"You lay here and don't try to move. I'm going to get a cold cloth and some water." Before she could protest, Gina had run back into the Inn. In a moment she reappeared and put the cool cloth on Kate's head and held her head up a little so she could get a drink of water.

"Can you move your arms and legs?" Gina asked.

"Yes, I'm fine. Just a little embarrassed that's all." Kate moved slowly, trying to focus her eyes.

Gina helped Kate to her feet and gently guided her over to the bench under the gazebo.

"Has this ever happened before?" Gina asked, not turning loose of Kate until she knew she was going to be all right.

"Not since I was nine and fell off of a horse," Kate admitted.

"Do you want me to take you to a doctor? There is one in town that I know would see you," Gina offered.

"No, I think I will be fine." Kate tried to sit very still.

"Maybe you should eat something," Gina suggested when she remembered Kate had not had anything except coffee that morning.

"Maybe that would be a good idea."

Gina helped Kate walk back into the kitchen and had her sit on a barstool while she prepared a snack for her. Gina was wishing Vivian was here; she was already getting behind in her work, but first things first, she reminded herself.

Kate ate some cheese and crackers and drank the orange juice Gina had given her. She was feeling better, but a little shaken. Gina was relieved to see the color coming back into her cheeks. She had taken first aid and CPR but really didn't want to ever have to use them. Gina noticed again the sadness that seemed to overwhelm Kate, the dark circles around her eyes, and the grief she could see in them. She didn't want to pry, but thought that maybe Kate needed someone to talk to.

"Kate, are you sure you don't want to go into town and have a doctor take a look at you? It wouldn't be any trouble, really," Gina offered again.

"No, I'm feeling better now." She tried to smile.

"So, this has not happened except once before in your entire life?" Gina asked.

"No… no it hasn't. It does seem a little strange," Kate admitted.

"The only person I've seen faint was my friend, Allison. She passed out cold while we were shopping one day. Turns out she was pregnant."

The look on Kate's face made Gina realize that what she had just said was obviously not the right thing. Kate began to sob uncontrollably. Gina went and got a box of tissues and handed them to her. She didn't know what to say. *Is she pregnant but doesn't want the baby?* Gina wondered. After a few minutes, Kate regained her composure.

"I'm so sorry! I'm sitting here crying like an idiot," Kate wailed as she blew her nose.

"It's fine. Anything you want to tell me?" Gina asked, as she put an arm around her shoulders.

"Where do I begin? My husband, Matt, and I have been trying to have a baby for more than three years. We have tried in vitro twice and fertility drugs and still no baby. He refuses to adopt. My marriage is in shambles, and Matt feels I need to put this behind me and move on to the next phase of our lives, whatever that means. I just can't seem to imagine the rest of my life without a child in it." Kate dabbed her eyes.

"I am so sorry. I don't know what to say," Gina said apologetically.

"It's okay. You didn't know my situation."

"This must be very difficult for you." Gina gave her shoulders a squeeze.

"That is why I'm here, to try and sort out what to do next and see how we can salvage our marriage. Matt is a good guy, but he has reached his limit. Maybe it means more to me than to him, or maybe he just hides his feelings better; I don't know. I have started seeing a therapist and that has helped some, but Matt refuses to go talk to anyone about it. I just really don't know what to do next," Kate blubbered as she sniffed loudly.

"Well, what did you like to do before you started trying to have a baby?" Gina asked. "Funny you should ask that, because I've been thinking about that since I got here. I know I want to get back into gardening. I used to really enjoy that. I have also been thinking about going back to school, maybe changing careers. Maybe I can do something where I help children in some way." Kate tried to smile, but the pain was still etched in her eyes.

"It sounds to me like you are on the right track," Gina offered, not sure how to help her.

"You know, it feels like someone very close to me has died. I know that sounds strange, but that is what it feels like to me." Kate sniffed and dabbed her eyes.

"That doesn't sound strange at all. Your dream has died, and sometimes that is the hardest thing of all to lose."

Chapter Six

Up in her room Maggie worked away at her computer. She had new inspiration and had started work on a short story. She was smiling to herself, when she noticed the clock read 11:30 a.m. With only thirty minutes to get ready before she was to meet Frank, she hit the save button on her computer and got up to try and figure out what to wear. She had only two outfits with her, as she always traveled light, so she decided to leave on what she already wore to breakfast. If she changed, Frank would think she was trying to impress him. She was, but she didn't want him to know that. She touched up her makeup, brushed her teeth again, and tried unsuccessfully to make her curls behave. She tucked some lipstick and a scarf into her purse and headed out the door. She felt silly for being excited about having lunch with Frank. He was a little uptight about life, but he was fun once he loosened up a bit, she decided.

She was trying not to compare him to Neal, but that was difficult. Neal was the ideal man, husband, and lover as far as Maggie was concerned. She realized that those things were rare, and one was lucky to find them once in a lifetime. She knew that nobody would ever measure up to Neal, so she needed to stop comparing every man to him. Still it was difficult not to.

In his room Frank had changed clothes for the second time. He had researched restaurants in the nearby town and had decided on a nice little café that served local favorites. He was proud of himself for making the decision. In the past they would have eaten wherever Carol wanted to eat. He realized that in some ways giving Carol all of the control had made his life easier. He only had to focus on his work and what Carol wanted. He didn't have to decide things for himself. It was as if Carol had taken over where his mother left off, and somehow he had become comfortable with that. As he looked at himself in the mirror he felt like a school boy, but he loved every minute. He put on a sports jacket and then took it off. He didn't want to appear stuffy. He put on some cologne and made his way to the lobby. He hoped he didn't look as nervous as he felt.

Frank was waiting in the lobby when he saw Maggie coming down the stairs. Her smile lit up her face and made him smile in return.

"Are you hungry?" Frank asked as Maggie got to the bottom of the stairs.

LISA SAMSON

"Starving! Would you like to ride in the convertible? I'll even let you drive." Maggie dangled the keys in front of him.

"I'd love to, but I'd prefer it if you drove. I haven't driven a stick in years, and I would hate to tear up your transmission." His remark made both of them laugh. They made their way to Maggie's car as Maggie pulled out a scarf and put it around her hair.

"Good idea, I wish I had thought of that." Frank couldn't believe in all of the things he packed, he didn't have a hat.

"I can lend you one of my scarves." Maggie laughed.

"I guess I should clarify. I wish I had brought a hat." Frank laughed too. "I researched restaurants in town, and I found one that sounded good. It said it served local favorites. How does that sound? If you want to go somewhere else, we can do that too," Frank added quickly.

"It sounds wonderful; just tell me where to go."

Frank and Maggie took a booth near the window at the restaurant. It was decorated in turquoise and terra cotta colors with a definite Southwest flavor. There were pottery and woven rugs in every corner, and it felt very cozy. They both ordered the special, which were enchiladas.

"Red, green, or Christmas tree?" the waitress asked. Frank looked puzzled.

"I'll have mine Christmas tree, just put his sauce on the side," Maggie told the waitress. Obviously Maggie had more experience with different foods than Frank.

He tended to order the same things at the same restaurants, and somehow Maggie must have sensed this about him.

"They have a green sauce and a red sauce, and one is spicier than the other. Christmas tree means they put both sauces on the food," Maggie explained as she took a sip of tea.

"Why didn't you order mine Christmas tree, like yours?" Frank asked.

"Because you don't strike me as a person who eats very spicy food, and I didn't want to ruin your lunch in case that was true. This way you can put on as much or as little as you like," Maggie grinned.

"So I guess I can safely say that you must like spicy food." Frank was a little embarrassed but grateful at the same time.

"I do. I enjoy trying the local fare whenever I travel."

Frank told Maggie about his job and his divorce from Carol. Maggie told stories of her life with Neal and all about their daughter, Elizabeth. Frank could tell she was extremely proud of her daughter. The food was delicious, and Frank was glad Maggie had gotten the sauce on the side. It was good, but a little bit was enough for him. He marveled at the way Maggie could eat such spicy food and not break into a sweat.

Frank couldn't believe it when he glanced at his watch and two hours had passed. He did not want their time together to end. He felt alive and excited about life for the first time in a long time. And finally Carol's voice was not the voice he heard in his mind.

Looking into Maggie's blue eyes melted his heart, and he thought that he could get very used to looking at them on a daily basis. He was trying not to think of the long term, but to live in the moment. It was difficult for him because he was a planner by nature, but Maggie was helping him see that you needed to enjoy every minute. He could not imagine the ordeal Maggie had lived through losing Neal. He was impressed by the fact that she was not bitter after all she had been through.

Frank felt like he had a new lease on life. He had not been this happy in such a long time; he couldn't stop smiling. Maggie was different from any woman he had ever met, and yet she was simple in many ways. She was genuine, and he felt instantly at ease around her. He hoped she felt the same way about him, but didn't want to push. It was early in their relationship, and he didn't want to scare her away. But he didn't know how long he could refrain from kissing her either.

Frank and Maggie decided to stroll around town and look at the local shops. There were a few antique stores, a pottery store, and a couple of local artists who had galleries with their work on display. The air was warm but not too hot, and there was a smell of red chilies in the air. People seemed to take their time and not be in such a hurry, and it made for a very pleasant atmosphere. Maggie was surprised to find that Frank was quite knowledgeable about antiques. She had purchased several antique furniture pieces when Neal was alive and still loved each one as much as the day she bought it. Neal never understood why you would want something old when you could afford new, but he hadn't complained when she brought the antique furniture home. Frank told Maggie that he had some unique antique pieces that he would like to show her sometime, which pleased her.

After a couple of hours of browsing, they bought some fresh lemonade from a street stand and sat on a bench near the end of the main street. The sky was a glorious blue, with just a few white clouds floating overhead. The air smelled fresh and there were little birds hopping nearby hoping for a crumb of food. It had been a wonderful afternoon, and they both had enjoyed it immensely.

"I guess I will be heading home in the morning." Maggie turned to face Frank.

"I need to be getting back to work, too." Frank admitted, although he may have stayed another day if Maggie was planning on staying. Suddenly the thought of not seeing her again made him feel like he couldn't catch his breath.

"Why don't you join me later in the week for one of my famous salmon dinners?"

"You cook! I'm impressed," Maggie beamed.

"Wait 'til you taste it; you will be even more impressed." Frank hoped that was true. He had taken up cooking mostly out of necessity after Carol left but found that he loved it. It relaxed him and brought out his creative side.

"Can I bring anything to dinner?" Maggie asked.

"Just yourself and maybe a bottle of wine. I'll give you directions when we get back to the Inn along with my phone number in case you need to reach me." Frank always thought of the practical things.

Maggie smiled as they walked back to her car. She had enjoyed the day more than she cared to admit. She had planned on writing more that afternoon, but decided that spending it with Frank had been much more fun. Frank held her hand as they walked back to the car. His hand was warm and softer than she had expected. She liked the way her hand fit in his, and it made her feel safe to be with him. Meeting Frank had been a sweet surprise. She only wished that the feelings of guilt she was having would go away.

Chapter Seven

Damian awoke slowly, struggling to determine exactly where he was. He had been dreaming of an operation they had been working on in the Marine Corps, and he felt disoriented. He rubbed his eyes and looked around the room. Sunlight streamed through the windows. *I should have shut the curtains*, he thought to himself. As he rolled over on his back, he noticed the skylight above his bed, and marveled at how it framed the sky beautifully. He watched a lone cloud move slowly across the blue expanse of sky, as he wondered what he should do next. He looked at the bedside clock, and it read 3:15 in the afternoon. He had slept most of the day, he realized. He was also very hungry. He dressed in jeans and a T-shirt and headed downstairs. Maybe he could find a place in town to grab a bite to eat.

When he rounded the corner at the bottom of the stairs, the aroma of food cooking overwhelmed his senses. It smelled of garlic and tomatoes, and his stomach began to rumble.

"Hi, there. Do you feel better after getting some sleep?" Damian looked up and saw Gina smiling at him. She was a pretty woman, with small features and a warm smile. Her golden hair fell loosely around her shoulders, and she wore just a hint of makeup. He liked that about her; he was never one to fall for a woman that wore a lot of make-up. It just seemed like they were trying to be something they weren't, and he didn't tolerate that well. She wore jeans and a tank top, with flip-flops on her feet. She looked completely at ease, not just with herself, but with her surroundings. He wondered if he would ever feel like that again.

"I feel much better, thank you. Except now I am starving and was hoping you could give me directions to a place where I could get some food," Damian said hopefully.

"No need for that. Dinner is included here, and I have some marinara sauce ready in the kitchen. If you can wait about ten minutes, I will make you some pasta." Gina didn't wait for a reply as she headed toward the kitchen.

"That would be great." Damian followed her into the kitchen and sat on one of the bar stools across from where she was working.

Gina was thinking about Kate, who had sat on that same bar stool a few hours ago. She made a mental note to check on her later. She put the pasta in the pot to cook and began slicing some French bread. She pulled a salad plate out of the fridge with fresh greens and tomatoes and sat it in front of Damian.

"What kind of dressing do you like?" she asked.

"Ranch would be fine," Damian replied.

"If you prefer to eat at the table instead of in the kitchen, you are welcome to."

Gina didn't want him to be uncomfortable with the informality of eating in the kitchen.

"This is fine, and I actually prefer it. I was never one for formal affairs. I probably wouldn't have a formal room in my house of any kind. I think a house should make you feel like you could live in any of the rooms, not save a room just for some special occasion."

Damian felt a twinge as he thought about the house that was now his, but felt so empty. Gina caught the look of pain in his eyes.

"I couldn't agree more. I think a house should be a home, a place where you feel safe, and can be yourself. It shouldn't look or feel like a museum."

Gina suddenly remembered the envelope she had found with his name on it. "By the way, I think you might have dropped this on your way upstairs." She handed him the letter that his mother had sent to his unit. It had his name and rank neatly written on the outside. "I thought maybe you were in the military, and the haircut kind of gave it away," Gina offered as an explanation.

"United States Marine Corps, the one and only." Damian smiled as he said it, and was pleased when Gina returned the smile.

Damian looked at the letter and then set it aside. He wasn't sure why he had even brought it with him, but he knew sooner or later he would have to open it. He thought maybe reading it in some place other than home might make it easier somehow. Gina served up a steaming plate of pasta just as he finished the salad. As he ate Gina sensed a determination about him. He wasn't one to give up or give in easily she guessed. Damian finished the huge plate of pasta and three slices of French bread.

"That was wonderful. Did you make the sauce yourself?" Damian wiped his mouth with his napkin.

"I did indeed, from vegetables I grew in my own garden," Gina said proudly.

"I'm impressed," replied Damian, and he meant it.

He wondered why he hadn't noticed Gina when he first met her. She was very cute and seemed like a genuine, kind person. He wondered why she was hiding in this little spot in the desert. Everyone has baggage, he realized, even him.

"Would you like some dessert? I have fresh lemon pie." She picked up his plate off the counter.

"I'll have to take a rain check. I am so full; I couldn't eat another bite right now. But give me a couple of hours, and you had better hide the pie." He flashed a grin, and Gina blushed just a little. *He has the cutest dimples,* she thought.

She also knew that being with a Marine would bring nothing but heartache and headaches. She couldn't imagine being with a man who at a moment's notice could be gone to the other side of the world to fight against terrorists and possibly never return. *How could you ever sleep at night?* One of her friends had married a man that was in the Navy. She was a single parent much of the time, because he was out at sea for months. Somehow Gina couldn't imagine a life like that. She was content in her desert oasis, running the Blue Moon, or at least that is what she told herself.

Damian went outside and sat down on the glider. It was a glorious day, and he felt a little guilty for sleeping so much of it away. He took the letter out of his pocket and ran his hand over it. He imagined his mom sealing the envelope and tried to remember the details of her face. It wasn't fair that she had died so suddenly, and he had to fight a wave of anger that surprised him. He couldn't imagine what was in the letter. All the details of the estate had been spelled out clearly and the attorney said everything was clear and straight forward. Maybe there was some hidden asset his mother wanted him to know about somewhere. Whatever was in the letter was obviously something his mother had gone to great lengths to make sure he received. He somehow sensed that it was something that was going to change his life in some way, but he had no idea what was in store for him. It made him sad to think that this was his last connection to his mom, the last thing from her that he had. Opening it would make her death seem real and final, the last piece of her life's puzzle.

Damian took a deep breath and tore open the envelope. There, in his mother's neat handwriting, were several pages. He checked the envelope to make sure there was nothing else inside, before dropping his eyes to read the words his mother had written to him.

My dearest Damian,

You have been the greatest joy of my life, and I am so glad that I got to be your mother. You are a wonderful person, and I am proud to be called your mom. I know if you are reading this that I must be gone. I know that will not be easy, but please don't mourn too long. I want you to go on and have a good life, full of all the things that make you happiest. There is something I need to tell you and am ashamed that I was too much of a coward to tell you when I was alive. I hope you can forgive me, and that in time you will understand why I kept this from you until now. So here it goes…

Before I married your Dad, I was in love with another man. He was one of the most kind and handsome men I had ever known. His name was David. He was home on leave from the Marine Corps when we met. I fell head over heels crazy in love with him. I know that is hard for you to imagine of your mother, but I was young once! We had a passionate few weeks together before he was to leave on his next deployment. He was going to Vietnam. Keep in mind, many of the men that were sent there never returned, and those that did were never the same. Anyway, a few weeks after he left, I discovered I was pregnant…with you. He had promised he would write to me, and he kept his promise. He said he wanted to marry me when he got back stateside. In the beginning I wrote to him every day, as we were very much in love. After I found out I was going to have you, I decided that I would not tell him until he returned home. I didn't want him to be distracted from the war. I wanted him to have a chance to come home alive. After a few months, his letters stopped coming. I assumed he was dead or missing in action. I waited and prayed, but the next letter I received from him was not until five years later. He had been taken as a prisoner of war and was unable to communicate with me or anyone back home. I had cried a river by then, but had moved on with my life.

I left home so as not to embarrass my parents. I bought a cheap wedding band and wore it and told everyone that my husband had been killed in the war. Unwed mothers were not as socially accepted back then. I took what little I had saved and got a small apartment and a job as a secretary. About two years after my last letter from David, I met your dad. He was wonderful to me and a great father to you. There is more to being a parent than biology, always remember that. Dad thought my husband had died in the war, and I just could never bring myself to tell him the truth. I didn't want him to think less of me. I loved your dad, and he loved you as his own. He was older than I, but he made me feel safe. He was not able to have children, so he was grateful he had you for a son. Anyway, when I finally heard from your biological father, I was already married and busy raising you. I decided it was best to leave the past in the past. I told him I had married someone else and now had a son. He was crushed and heartbroken. He said I was what had helped keep him alive all those years in the POW camp. I felt terrible, but to tell the truth then would have destroyed your dad and confused you.

Over the years, as I watched you grow, it made me sad that David had missed all of that. He was a wonderful man, and I know he would have loved you very much. I had heard through the grapevine that he had married briefly, but that military life had been too difficult for his wife and they divorced. To my knowledge he had one daughter. Imagine my surprise when you told me you wanted to join the Marine Corps! Before I wrote this letter to you, I also wrote one to David. I didn't want to go to my grave with this secret. I told David in my letter how sorry I was to have deprived him of getting to know you, his son. I also explained why I had stopped waiting for him to return, but if I had somehow kept him alive, then I was grateful for that. I can only hope that he can forgive me and you as well. David's last name is Alexander, and the last I knew he was still serving in the Marine Corps. I don't know how you or he will feel about all of this, but I hope some good can come out of it. I love you, Damian, and I can only hope that one day you will understand. Please don't hate me. I never intended for this to hurt you. I just felt that I finally owed you the truth. You have been one of the greatest joys of my life. Remember, even if you can't see me, I will be with you.

Love Always,
Mom

Damian sat with his mouth open as he tried to absorb what his mother had told him. He tried to imagine his mother being so young and in love and then all alone and unwed with a baby on the way. He thought of his dad and wondered why he had never told him the truth. Maybe he was doing as his mother had asked; maybe he was embarrassed that he could not father children of his own.

The warm desert breeze blew across his face as he sat there, too much in shock to move. David Alexander was his real father and he had a half sister somewhere. He wondered why he had not tried to find him. Damian would be able to access his information in the Marine Corps data base if he were still alive. If he was about the same age as his mother, he would be around fifty.

Suddenly the realization of who his father might be overwhelmed him. Could it be that his father was Colonel Alexander? The one he had come to trust so much after his mother's death? If so, why didn't he say something to him if he had gotten a letter from his mother too? No, it was impossible. The odds that he had served with his real father were next to none. It had to be coincidence that the colonel had the same name as his father.

Damian didn't know what to feel or think. Did he really want to know this man who was his biological father? Did his father really want to know him? He certainly wouldn't feel so alone in the world if he actually had a dad and sister in his life. But what if they didn't want to know him? How could his mom have lived her whole life with this secret? He felt it had been very unfair, not only to him, but to everyone involved. He tried to imagine how his mother must have felt and why she had chosen to keep the truth from him. The grief he felt was now replaced by anger, but at least that was more familiar to him. He clenched his teeth and his fists and began pacing around the backyard of the Inn. He finally turned and went inside.

He passed Gina on his way into the Inn, and she could see by the look on his face, that he was terribly upset.

"Damian, is everything all right?" Gina asked as Damian rushed past her.

"No, it isn't, not at all," he managed through gritted teeth. "I need a little time to think. If it is all right with you, I'd like to stay here again tonight. I'll leave in the morning." Damian tried to avert her gaze.

"That's fine; stay as long as you need to. Anything I can help with?" Gina asked cautiously.

"Not unless you can bring my mother back from the grave." Damian pushed past Gina and took the stairs two at a time and ran to his room. Gina stood there wondering what had happened. *Surely he didn't just find out that his mother had passed away, but what else could it be?* Maybe he would feel like talking about it, but, then again, she sensed that talking was not his usual way of handling things.

Chapter Eight

After a nap Kate was feeling better. She decided to drive down to the local flea market and have a look around. She was surprised by how many vendors were selling home-grown vegetables. Maybe that was something she could do if she ever got her garden going again. There were also women selling large hand-made tapestries in vibrant colors. The smell of red chilies and sage were in the air, and occasionally a dog would wander by taking in all the sights and sounds.

Kate saw a woman pushing a stroller with a little girl in it. The little girl looked to be about nine months old and had pink ribbons in her short, dark hair. Kate felt that familiar twinge of longing well up inside her. Would it ever get any easier? Surely she wouldn't feel this way every time she saw a baby for the rest of her life. *Just think about something else*, she told herself.

She stopped at another booth to look at the colorful handbags. She purchased one and then moved to the next booth. It was filled with baby quilts for sale. Kate felt a lump in her throat as she quickly passed by. She didn't know how much more she could take today.

She decided to get herself some iced tea and then sat on a bench, enjoying the sunshine. She knew she should probably call Matt, but she just wasn't ready yet. She thought she would stay another day or two and then head back to Phoenix. The fainting spell she had earlier in the day had concerned her a little. She finally decided it was probably due to stress and lack of food, and was not planning on telling Matt about the incident. She had been poked and prodded enough to last a lifetime and was not eager to go back to the doctor. A small wave of nausea came over her again, but then left just as quickly as it had come. She wondered if maybe she needed some vitamins.

Kate finished her tea and made her way back to her car. She was glad she hadn't parked too far away, as she was suddenly feeling very tired. When she got into her car, she laid her head back against the seat and closed her eyes. She was surprised when she woke up fifteen minutes later. She decided that she definitely needed to take some vitamins. She hadn't eaten well in the past few weeks and had lost five pounds without even trying. Again, she assured herself it was due to stress and tension, and pushed the symptoms out of her mind as she drove back to the Blue Moon.

Vivian was busy in the kitchen finishing the dinner preparations. "Don't bother setting anything out for Damian, he already ate dinner a little earlier," Gina told Vivian as she sat a vase of freshly cut flowers down on the counter.

"Giving him the special treatment, huh?" Vivian grinned.

"Just being a good hostess, that's all," Gina replied without looking her in the eye.

"Come on, G, you can't tell me you haven't noticed how cute he is, especially when those dimples appear." Gina blushed, but turned so Vivian couldn't see her.

"I guess I didn't notice," Gina lied. "Besides, he is in the Marine Corps, so there is no point in pursuing that. God, Corps, and Country, no room for a serious woman," Gina said sarcastically.

"There are a lot of people in the military that are married, and they find a way to make it work," Vivian said.

"Well, I am not going to settle for someone who has given his heart to Uncle Sam. If I ever get married, I want to have his full attention." Gina sighed as she began to empty the dishwasher.

"Billy Woods would marry you in a heartbeat, but you won't give him the time of day," Vivian shot back at her. "And he is not in the military."

"Billy Woods would marry any woman that wore a skirt, drank beer and threw darts. He spends more time at the pool hall than he does at work. That is not what I would consider husband material. Besides, I am perfectly happy as I am. I don't need a man to be fulfilled," Gina said defiantly.

"Whatever you say." Vivian grinned.

Dinner at the Inn that night was fun. Kate was looking better and ate most of her salad and pasta. She even had a small slice of lemon pie for dessert. She made an effort to join in the conversation and actually smiled a few times during dinner. *A big improvement over a few days ago*, Gina thought. Frank and Maggie seemed very at ease with each other. Frank actually was telling stories that made the women laugh until they cried. He was quite funny; maybe Gina had him pegged all wrong. Either that or Maggie was bringing out the best in him, which was probably more the case.

Maggie was telling stories of her writing on the road. She once traveled across the country interviewing homeless people for a story she was doing. She said it was one of the scariest, yet most interesting things she had ever done. She couldn't imagine ever letting her daughter do something like that, but yet she hadn't thought twice about her safety when she was in the middle of it all.

Everyone loved the lemon pie, and Gina told them it had been her mother's recipe. She had saved a piece for Damian and thought maybe she would take it up later and see if he was interested in eating it. She was curious as to what had upset him so much, but she didn't want to pry, at least not too much.

After dinner Frank and Maggie went to sit in the gazebo. They invited Kate to join them, but she said she needed to make a phone call and headed up to her room. Vivian and Gina cleaned up the dishes, and then Vivian went home. Gina was going to retreat to her room, but thought maybe she would take a piece of pie up to Damian and see if he was doing better than the last time she saw him.

Gina had a large bedroom and private bath on the main floor. It had an old bathtub with claw feet, and she loved to soak in it with lots of bubbles. She had decorated her room in soft pinks and white lace, and she loved it. It was a peaceful retreat yet it was close enough that if any of the guests needed anything, she was near. She would have to wait until she checked on Damian before retiring to her room she decided, even though she was very tired.

In his room Damian was pacing the floor. He felt like a caged animal but yet didn't know what else to do except continue pacing and try to think. He had decided that he was not going to contact Colonel Alexander. If he knew that he was his father then he must not want to own up to it or have anything more to do with him. But, somehow, deep down Damian knew that the colonel would not react that way if given the facts. He was one of the most honest and loyal men he had ever met, and if in fact he was his father, then Damian should take some comfort in that. But if he knew, why hadn't he said anything? Maybe he thought it would upset his daughter too much to learn she suddenly had a brother. He had heard the colonel mention his daughter a couple of times, as best as he could remember she was about nineteen and going to college somewhere on the East Coast. His thoughts were interrupted by a knock on the door.

He opened the door to find Gina standing there holding a piece of lemon pie. "I saved you a slice of pie. If you don't want it now you could save it for later." Gina held out the plate to him. Damian gave her a half smile. She looked so cute standing there with her long hair pulled neatly back in a pony tail. Her toenails sported a hot pink color and her legs were longer than he had remembered.

"Thank you. Do you want to come in for a minute?" Damian took the pie and put it on the night stand as Gina came in and sat in the chair by the window. "I'm sorry I was so abrupt with you earlier." He sighed as he sat down on the bed.

"It's okay. It sounded like you got some shocking news." She swung one leg over the other, and Damian had to force himself to concentrate.

"You could say that."

Damian decided to go out on a limb and trust her. He really didn't have anybody else at the moment, and he needed an objective opinion. He explained to her about his mother's death in the car accident and then all about the letter. Gina sat and listened to the whole story with wide eyes. She easily understood now why he had been so upset. When Damian had finished the story he fell back on the bed, exhausted from the whole ordeal.

"What do you think I should do?" Damian asked as he looked into her eyes. Her eyes were clear and bright green with little flecks of gold he noticed.

"Wow that is a lot of information to digest. I guess I would say that you are probably a very good judge of character. So if you think highly of Colonel Alexander, then I am sure he must be a very decent man. You don't know if, in fact, he is your father. There could be another David Alexander in the Marine Corps." Gina paused but decided to continue. "But I think that you will always wonder about the man that is your father if you don't make an effort to find him. Time is precious, and you don't know what the future holds. I think you both have missed out on too much to give up the chance to get to know this man and possibly a sister. What do you have to lose?" Gina asked.

"But what if he doesn't want to open that can of worms? What if he thinks it is better to let the past stay in the past, and doesn't want a relationship with me?" Damian began to pace again.

"Well, then, at least you will know. And you won't be any worse off than you are right now. But if he wants to get to know you, then you would be missing out on maybe one of the best relationships of your life." Gina paused as she looked him in the eye. Damian glanced away. He couldn't believe he had bared his soul to a total stranger. He hoped she didn't think he was strange for talking to her this way.

"Thanks for listening, I really appreciate it." He stopped pacing and turned toward her.

"Anytime. Why don't you sleep on it, and let me know in the morning what you're thinking. A good night's sleep can often change everything." Gina gave Damian a quick little hug and then shut the door behind her. If he hadn't been so distraught, he would have been thinking about how wonderful her hair smelled when she hugged him.

In her room, Kate was trying to decide what to say to Matt if she called him. She had a wave of nausea and felt a little light headed for a moment, so she sat down on the edge of the bed. She decided that maybe she would take Gina up on her offer and see if she would recommend a doctor in town. She decided to just have things checked out before she went home, that way she wouldn't have to tell Matt. She was sure he was tired of her going to the doctor all the time anyway. She was so tired lately, maybe she was anemic.

She called Matt on their home phone but only got the answering machine, so decided to try his cell. He picked it up on the third ring.

"Hey, thought maybe you had forgotten about me," he said with a little accusation in his voice.

"The phone lines go both ways." Kate instantly regretted that she had been so cynical. She didn't want to argue with Matt anymore. It was just too draining.

LISA SAMSON

"Sorry. I've just been doing some thinking, trying to figure out what to do next," Kate said with a sigh.

"Any ideas?" Matt said hopefully.

"Well, I don't have the rest of my life planned if that's what you mean. I have decided I need to get back to doing some things I used to enjoy, like gardening. I've also been thinking about changing jobs or going back to school." Kate frowned as she lay back on the bed.

"I think that is a good idea. You never loved your job at the bank anyway. I think you should open a flower shop. You love to garden and have such a way with flowers." Kate was surprised that Matt had given this some thought too, and she had to admit, she sort of liked his idea.

"Well, I'm still thinking about it, but I appreciate you being open to some possibilities. I think I will stay another day or two and then head home." Kate swallowed hard as she stared up at the sky.

"Take as long as you need." Kate was surprised to find tears on her cheeks. It seemed like she cried all the time now. She had read that pregnant women were more emotional, she couldn't imagine how much worse she would be if she had ever become pregnant.

"Take care...and Matt" Kate paused.

"Yeah" Matt replied.

"I love you."Kate wiped the tears away with the back of her hand.

"I love you too. Everything is going to be all right, just wait and see," Matt said softly. After hanging up

the phone, Kate laid back on the bed. The sun was setting and the sky was a glorious blend of oranges and
pinks. For the first time in a long time, she actually felt
like there was hope for the future.

Gina was unable to sleep. She had tried taking a bubble
bath to help her relax but she just couldn't stop thinking
about Damian and the letter. She couldn't imagine getting such shocking news, but to have it delivered to you
after your mother died was incomprehensible. She tried
to imagine why his mother had not told him the truth
when she was alive. It seemed like a coward's way out
to put it in a letter to only be delivered after she died.
His mother had deprived Damian and his father of the
chance to know each other and have a real relationship.
She could understand not telling him while her husband had been alive, but his mother at least could have
told him after he passed away. Maybe there were things
his mother knew that he didn't, but she had a feeling
Damian was going to try and find his father.

Gina was grateful both of her parents were still living. They came to visit every few months, usually on
their way to some new adventure in their RV. Since
they had retired they liked to travel around the country seeing the sights. They met up with her aunt and
uncle from time to time at different campsites, which
was fun for them. She was happy they were able to do
it, and it made it easier for her if they came to see her.

LISA SAMSON

Vivian could run the Inn for her for a few days, but she didn't really feel right leaving it for very long. Gina had a younger brother, Chris, but he was busy finishing his degree at USC.

Gina lay in bed and thought about Damian. He was very nice looking, and she thought he was a genuinely nice person. It surprised her a little that he opened up to her so easily. His eyes were blue with long, dark lashes. He had muscles in all the right places, obviously the Marine Corps kept him in great shape. His smile is what got to her the most. His dimples would pop out and his whole face would look as if he could break into laughter. Just thinking about it made her smile. She realized she was going down a dangerous path. He would soon be gone, and Uncle Sam would have him back. There just wasn't room for her in his world, so she should not even think about it. But try as she might, Damian's smile was the last thing on her mind as she finally drifted off to sleep.

Chapter Nine

Kate made her way downstairs to talk to Gina about recommending a doctor for her. She was feeling nauseous again this morning and even though she thought it was nothing serious, she knew she would feel better if a doctor confirmed it. "Good morning, Kate," Gina greeted her as she came into the dining room. Gina noticed right away that Kate was a little pale again. "How are you feeling?"

"Not the best. I was hoping you could recommend a doctor in town for me to see. I don't think it is anything serious, probably just a virus or something." Kate looked around uncomfortably as she sat down on the couch.

"Let me make a phone call, and I'll be right back."

Gina went into the kitchen and called the local clinic. They were very good about seeing the occasional guest from the Inn, and Gina was grateful.

"I made an appointment for you at two o'clock this afternoon with Dr. Taylor." She gave Kate directions to the clinic and then offered her some coffee or juice. "You better eat something. I don't want you fainting again," Gina reminded her. Kate agreed to coffee and toast. She felt a little better after she ate it, although those first few bites were hard to get down. She decided to go sit in the garden outside and enjoy the rest of her coffee. It was so peaceful with the fountain and the birds singing. It made Kate want to sit there for hours.

Maggie and Frank arrived at the dining room about the same time. They were already engrossed in a conversation about fly fishing when Gina began bringing the food into the room. They were going home today, and it made both of them a little sad. Maggie had worked on her new article until midnight, but was pleased with the progress she was making. Frank had stayed up and watched an old western in black and white, while packing his suitcase. He was looking forward to his dinner date with Maggie on Friday, and had made a list of the things he needed to do to prepare for it. He just felt more in control if he was organized, and he decided that it was not a flaw but rather an asset depending on how you looked at it.

Gina brought in bowls of scrambled eggs made with peppers from her garden. Along with the eggs, Gina served toast, breakfast potatoes, fresh fruit, and, of course, a large supply of coffee. Gina believed quality was in the details and even ground her own coffee beans. She kept waiting for Damian to come down for breakfast, but had not seen him. Maybe he decided to sleep in this morning. If he had slept as poorly as she had, she could understand it. She hoped she could grab a short nap later in the day. She was already tired.

After breakfast Maggie and Frank checked out of the Inn and walked to their cars. They were both sad to go, but were excited that they would be seeing each other later in the week. Frank gave Maggie directions to his house and his phone number. Maggie gave her number to Frank as well and promised to bring a bottle of wine to dinner on Friday. So far, they had not done anything more intimate than hold hands. Frank had been debating about whether he should kiss her good-bye. He didn't want to appear too pushy and scare her away. It had been so long since he had been on the dating scene he didn't know what was acceptable these days. He wondered if Maggie had dated much since Neal passed away, but he got the feeling that she had not.

"Well, I have really enjoyed the time we have spent together. I'm looking forward to seeing you on Friday." Frank smiled as he opened the trunk on Maggie's car so she could put her bag in it.

"I've had a nice time, too. And I've been able to get the writer's juices flowing again, which was the point of this trip for me in the beginning."

Maggie turned and gave Frank a quick hug and then hopped into her convertible. With a wave, she was off. The wind was blowing her hair and her blue eyes were shielded behind big sunglasses. He got in his car, which suddenly seemed boring to him after riding with Maggie. He headed toward home and was feeling better than he had in months. He felt as though he had turned a corner somehow, and that the future wasn't such a scary place after all.

Maggie drove around the curves and up and down the hills with the wind in her face. She realized that she had not stopped smiling. Part of her felt guilty about that, but part of her felt more like the old Maggie than she had in a long time. She thought about Frank. He was different from Neal, not as confident or impulsive, but he seemed safe and stable to her, and she liked that. Maybe that is exactly what she needed now. She thought about the way her hand felt in his. He was smart and could be quite funny once he relaxed a little.

She was curious to see what his house looked like. She imagined it to be very neat and clean with warm wood tones. Somehow modern didn't describe Frank. She began thinking about what she would wear on Friday. That was a surprise to her too, because usually she didn't plan for anything that was more than a day in advance unless it required booking a flight. She thought about her new article and was pleased that she was getting back to her writing; it made her feel more normal somehow. For months she had just sort of wandered through each day without much of a purpose, now she was ready to get back to the land of the living. She felt a little guilty, as if moving on was betraying Neal in some way. But she knew in her heart, he would have wanted her to get on with her life, and he had told her that in no uncertain terms before he died. She wondered if she would be lucky enough to find love a second time.

Damian was startled to see that he had slept past nine o'clock. He had not slept well, but thought he must have dozed off somewhere around two in the morning. He showered and dressed quickly and was hoping Gina had something he could eat for breakfast, because he was famished. He had eaten the slice of lemon pie the night before and thought it was very good. He took the plate and fork with him downstairs and found Gina in the kitchen.

"Good morning sleepy head." Gina flashed him a smile that said she was only teasing. "I have a feeling you didn't get the best night's sleep."

"You are right about that. Am I too late for breakfast?" Damian hopped up on a bar stool.

"I saved you a plate; just let me reheat it for you. Coffee?"

"Yes, please."

Gina took out a cup and poured steaming hot coffee in it. She already knew he liked it black. He just didn't seem the type that would like flavored coffee.

Damian grabbed the cup and took a sip. He stared out the window but didn't really see what was beyond the glass. The beeping of the microwave brought him back to reality.

"I've made a decision," he said boldly. Gina raised her eyebrows as if to ask what it was. "I've decided I am going to try and figure out who my biological father really is. It occurred to me that it is possible he may have passed away too." Damian didn't waste any time eating the eggs and potatoes Gina had placed before him.

"I think that is a very good idea. Where are you going to start?"

"The first thing I'm going to do is check the Marine Corps data base and see how many people by the name of David Alexander they have listed. Then I guess I'll just go from there." Damian finished his coffee, and Gina reached for the coffee pot.

"I would really like to know how things turn out. Do you think you could call me and let me know?" She hoped that wasn't asking too much, but she just had to know. Damian smiled. He thought that had to be one of the most original ways he ever got a girl's number.

"I'll let you know. Better yet, I'll be passing through this way on my way to my next duty station in California; maybe I will stop by and tell you in person." He flashed her one of his smiles.

"I'd like that." Gina felt herself blushing. "I'm from California. If you'd like, I can give you some tips on places to see and things to do."

"That would be appreciated. I went to California once when I was about ten years old, and that is the extent of my experience."

Gina laughed. She liked that he was not trying to impress her by acting like he knew more than he really did.

Damian finished his breakfast while he and Gina talked about California. She thought the distraction would do him good. He went upstairs to gather his things and then came to check out. Gina was sad to see him go, but she kept telling herself he was not what she needed. "Thank you for everything. I promise I will let you know how it turns out." Gina handed him a piece of paper with her phone number on it. His smile dazzled her, and she felt her cheeks turning red again.

"I will be anxiously waiting to hear all about it." Gina hoped that didn't sound like she would be sitting around waiting for the phone to ring or for him to come through the door.

Kate was nervous as she walked into the doctor's office. It was a small, old building with wood paneling on one wall. An elderly lady with gray hair greeted her and asked her to fill out insurance forms. Kate was feeling a little better. She had eaten part of a sandwich and a banana for lunch, which seemed to have set well with her. She returned the clipboard after completing the forms and then took a seat in the corner. There were several children in the small waiting area, and one of them was crying loudly as his mother tried to comfort him.

Finally they called Kate's name, and she followed the nurse back to the exam room. The nurse introduced herself as Lucy and proceeded to check her vital signs and get a brief medical history. Lucy didn't comment when Kate told her of the fertility drugs she had been on recently. "Have you ever been pregnant?"

Kate swallowed hard to fight back the tears before she spoke. "No, no I haven't." Lucy stood then and gave Kate a hospital gown and asked her to put it on with the opening to the back.

"Dr. Taylor will be in shortly." Without another word she turned and left the room, closing the door behind her.

Kate imagined Dr. Taylor to be an elderly man with thick glasses. She was pleasantly surprised when the door opened and a young, professional looking woman walked in and introduced herself as Dr. Taylor. She proceeded to examine Kate after a brief discussion about her symptoms. When she was finished, she told Kate to go ahead and sit up and get dressed, she would be back in a few minutes and they would talk about the next step.

When Dr. Taylor returned, she told Kate that so far her exam looked fine, but she wanted to run a couple of lab tests that would give her some more detailed information. She asked Kate for a phone number where she could be reached so she could call her once the test results were back. She assured her they should have them back by the end of the next day. Kate was relieved to hear that, as she wanted to get back home before the end of the week. Dr. Taylor walked Kate to the waiting area and told her she would be in touch.

Kate left a urine sample and they drew two tubes of blood. *This all seems so routine now,* Kate thought. She was tired of doctors' offices, she decided. She drove back to the Inn and went to sit outside on the glider. Gina had left some lemonade on the patio, and she poured herself a glass before sitting down.

Gina came out a few minutes later. "Back already, I see."

"Yes, they got me in right away. Dr. Taylor was very nice. She said it was probably a virus, but ran some lab tests anyway and said she will call me tomorrow." Kate took a sip of her lemonade.

"How are you feeling?" Gina sat down next to Kate on the glider.

"Right now, I feel fine. It's just strange, the symptoms seem to come and go."

"Well, I'm sure if there is something wrong, Brooke will figure it out," Gina reassured her.

"Sounds like you know Dr. Taylor very well."

"We went to college together in California. She then transferred to Harvard for medical school. She was always at the top of her class." Kate looked surprised.

"I know what you're thinking. Why would a doctor with those kinds of credentials want to come to this area to practice medicine?"

"Well, yes." Kate laughed a little awkwardly.

"Brooke fell in love with the desert in the Southwest. She loves the indigenous people and has done an extensive amount of research on diabetes. That is one of the diseases that seem to plague the natives here. By practicing here she also has time to continue her research on diabetes, which is her passion. She says they are closer all the time to a cure, and she wants to be a part of that."

"I'm impressed," Kate admitted. Kate told Gina she had expected an elderly male doctor with thick glasses, and Gina laughed.

"I guess I should have warned you."

Kate spent the afternoon reading outside on the glider. She had almost finished the book she had brought with her. She loved the tranquility of the garden and had taken special notice of the types of plants there so she could use some of them in her garden when she got home.

She had been giving some serious thought to what Matt had said and wondered why she had never thought of that before. A flower shop would be wonderful. With her business background, she felt certain she could manage the financial side easily and work alone for the first year or so until she got her business off the ground. Maybe she could find an existing flower shop to buy with a customer base already.

She had done the flowers for her own wedding and for several of her friends and really enjoyed it. She found herself smiling thinking of the possibility. Now if only she could decide on a name for her flower shop...

Chapter Ten

Damian had gotten in his car and decided to head back home. At least from there he could access a computer and a phone and try to figure out how to best go about searching for his father. He was less angry at his mother than he had been the day before, but he still felt a little guilty for being angry at a dead person in the first place. He also wondered if she had not died, if she would have decided to tell him the truth anyway. He would never know the answer to that question.

He found himself thinking of Gina and wondering what she was doing. It had surprised him that he felt so at ease with her. He liked the way she was so genuine and caring. Of course her long legs and green eyes were great too, he had to admit. He wondered if she had a boyfriend. He truly planned to stop and see her on his way to Camp Pendleton and found he was already missing her.

He could still smell a hint of his mother's perfume in the car. She had worn it since he was a child, and whenever he smelled it, he always thought of her. He could sense her presence somehow with him in this car. Even the radio was set to all of her favorite oldie stations. He didn't mind; he had grown to like the music, and he thought it probably reminded her of her youth. He wondered again if she had suffered before she died. This question he would have to leave unanswered. He hoped that when you got to heaven you suddenly had all of the answers to the questions you couldn't answer on earth. Or maybe those questions wouldn't matter there. His mom had been a woman of faith, and it gave him comfort to think of her in heaven now.

Gina was busy snapping green beans when Vivian came into the kitchen.

"Kind of quiet around here." Vivian plopped a basket of strawberries on the counter.

"It's always busier here on the weekends, but Kate is still here and there were two other couples that checked in earlier today. I'm making some chicken cordon bleu for dinner with some fresh green beans on the side."

"Smells great. I always eat better here than at home," Vivian teased. Gina knew that wasn't true. It was just that at Vivian's house they ate more traditional foods like tamales. She had them at the Inn sometimes too,

LISA SAMSON

but not all of her guests liked spicy food, so she tried to have a variety.

Gina had been thinking about Damian and wondering where he was. She knew he was headed back to Colorado. She scolded herself for daydreaming about him and tried to concentrate on the green beans.

When Damian returned home, he was surprised to find a message on the machine from Colonel Alexander. Could it be that he had gotten the letter from his mother too? Maybe something had changed with his orders, and he needed to report in earlier, he thought. Damian called the colonel at the number he had left on the machine.

"Hello," came the deep voice on the other end.

"Colonel Alexander?"

"Yes."

"This is Captain Roberts. You had left me a message to call you, sir." Damian paced up and down the hall as he talked.

"Yes, I did. How are you doing now that you are back in Colorado on leave?" The colonel cleared his throat.

"I'm managing, sir. It's hard, but I think I'm handling things." Damian forced himself to sit down.

"Glad to hear it. I'm back stateside myself now. I was planning a trip to Denver to attend a conference on strategic planning. I was hoping maybe we could meet for lunch or dinner toward the end of the week."

Damian froze. Was the colonel his father? If so, what would he say to him? "That would be fine, sir. I'm pretty free anytime, so whatever will work best with your schedule." *Just breathe*, he kept telling himself.

"Fine. I will have my secretary call you with a time and place for us to meet. You have my number if anything should change."

"Yes, sir, I look forward to seeing you."

Damian lay back on the couch. He felt a little dizzy thinking about it all. Maybe his father had been there all the time, and fate had allowed them to serve together in the Corps. Was it coincidence that he joined the Marine Corps, or could that possibly be genetic somehow? Another question he would have to leave unanswered. He had researched the Marine Corps data base and found three people with the name David Alexander. One had already passed away, and the other one only listed the unit he had been assigned to previously. The last one had been Colonel Alexander. At least it was a place to start.

Damian considered calling Gina with the news. He decided to wait until he had something really concrete to tell her. Having dinner with the colonel would hardly qualify as finding his father, at least not yet. He had carefully put her phone number in his wallet, so as not to lose it and also programmed it into his cell phone. Now, if only he could keep busy until the end of the week.

The next day, he decided to try and go through some of his mother's things and box up what he wanted to keep. He knew that he didn't want to rent the house, so if he decided to sell it, at least most of the things he wanted would be ready to be put in storage. His parents had a few nice antiques that he wanted to keep. Of course all of the pictures, his baby album, and the hope chest his grandfather had made he was going to keep as well. As far as the furniture, he didn't really have a need for it. If he ever got a place of his own, he wanted to decorate it with his own style. Most of the furniture was twenty years old or more, so he decided he might just donate it. He found some boxes in the garage and got to work. It was a bittersweet task. Everything held a memory, but he found that comforting too. Again, he seemed to sense his mother with him, and for the first time in months, he felt peaceful.

Damian worked until well past dark. He realized this was going to take him much longer than he had planned. It seemed everything he touched had some sort of memory attached to it, and to put it away without remembering just seemed wrong. He had laughed and cried off and on all afternoon. He found himself talking to his parents out loud, and afterward he began to wonder if this was normal.

He had made some substantial progress. He had managed to go through everything in the garage, guest bedroom, and office. He had a shred box, a huge box of things to donate, and boxes marked save. He also had found some legal papers and receipts in the office that he intended on discussing with the attorney. He didn't want to throw anything out that might be important. He was grateful that his parents were not pack rats and had done a decent job of keeping things in order.

He suddenly realized how hungry he was and decided to order a pizza. He didn't like to eat alone in the empty house, but he didn't feel like going out either. He was tired but was afraid he wouldn't be able to sleep even if he went to bed.

After finishing the pizza, he thought about calling Gina. He didn't know why he kept thinking of her. Maybe it was because he felt all alone now. Maybe it was because she was the only one he had trusted with the news of his biological father. She seemed as beautiful on the inside as the outside. She was genuine and he liked that very much. It would have surprised him to know that Gina had been thinking of him almost as much since he left the Inn.

Damian found himself on the couch when he awoke. The sun was streaming in through the window. He squinted to see what time it was; the clock read seven o'clock in the morning. He went to brush his teeth, because his mouth tasted like beer and pepperoni. As he went past the kitchen, he saw that there was a piece of pizza left in the box. He decided to call it breakfast and ate it before going down the hall to shower.

He worked all day trying to sort through things in the house. He put on some of his favorite music and was grateful for the distraction. He kept wondering if Colonel Alexander was really his father. They had the same color eyes, but that certainly wasn't conclusive. He tried to imagine what the colonel might have looked like when he was younger, but it was hard for him to come up with an image in his mind. He sincerely liked Colonel Alexander, and if he was in fact his son, he would be honored.

He would always be grateful to his dad, and nothing would ever diminish the love he had for him. He had been a wonderful father, but because he died before Damian had even graduated from high school, many of his memories of him were of when he was older. It was hard for him to play football or catch with him, but he tried his best. Other kids at school used to make fun of Damian's dad. "You coined the phrase 'old man'," they would say.

Damian had even gotten into a fight at school once because of the teasing. When his Dad came to the principal's office, Damian didn't have the heart to tell him the real reason he had punched Reggie Smith in the nose. His dad had been so disappointed in him for fighting, that he had been grounded in addition to the punishment he received at school. Still he knew it would have broken his dad's heart if had known the other kids were making fun of him because his dad was old.

Damian had always thought his parents were happy together. As they grew older, the difference in their age became more apparent. His dad was sixteen years older than his mom and was not in good health the last years of his life. When he was younger they would vacation in the mountains or go to the ocean. But as he got older, it was harder for his dad to travel and his mom spent a large portion of her time caring for him. She never complained, but he could tell there was weariness in her eyes. He wondered if she had dreamed of what her life would have been like if she had waited for his father. Not that she didn't, but after a while he could see why she gave up hope. He wondered if he would ever find a woman that would be able to withstand military life. He had a few buddies who were married, and it was a real struggle sometimes.

After finishing packing up the family room, Damian decided to check his messages. Sure enough there was a message from Colonel Alexander's secretary asking him to meet the colonel for dinner at a place called Rogers. She gave the address and asked him to let her know if he was unavailable. Damian wrote down the address and tucked it in his wallet next to Gina's number. He wouldn't miss this dinner for anything in the world.

Chapter Eleven

Kate was busy packing her clothes when her cell phone rang. She sat down on the bed to take the call, because she was feeling some nausea again. "Kate, this is Dr. Taylor." Kate was a little surprised that she had called herself instead of her nurse. She hoped this didn't mean that she had some really bad news.

"Hi, Dr. Taylor," she said softly.

"Kate, I have your test results back. You don't have a virus, and you aren't anemic."

"Well, that's good news, but what is wrong with me?" Kate felt herself almost begin to cry. Was she imagining things now?

"Actually, there is nothing wrong with you. But you are pregnant."

Kate sat in silence.

"Kate, did you hear me? I said you are going to have a baby. Congratulations!"

"Oh, Dr. Taylor, are you sure? We've been trying for so long; I had given up hope!"

"Yes, I'm sure. I suggest you get in touch with your doctor at home right away, so you can begin prenatal care. You will want to start on some prenatal vitamins right away."

"Yes… yes I will be sure and do that. Thank you so much, Dr. Taylor." Kate sat on the bed and cried and laughed all at the same time.

"Gina! Gina!" Kate called through the kitchen.

"I'm out on the patio." Gina was working in her vegetable garden. She looked up as Kate came through the door. "Wow, you look like you won the lottery," Gina smiled as she looked at Kate.

"Better than that. Dr. Taylor just called and said I'm not sick at all. She said I'm pregnant!" Gina jumped to her feet and threw her arms around Kate. They hugged and jumped up and down with excitement.

"Oh my gosh, that is the best news! Have you told Matt yet?" Gina asked with a huge smile on her face.

"No, I guess he should have been the person I told first, but I just had to tell someone in person. You've helped me so much, just by listening. Thank you for everything." Gina hugged Kate again.

"You better send me a picture once the baby is born."

"I will. It has been such a long road to get here, that I don't want to get my hopes up too much in case something happens. But I am so excited; my prayers have been answered. I'm heading home now, but I'll keep in touch." Gina walked Kate to her car. She

LISA SAMSON

wouldn't even let her carry her suitcase, which made Kate laugh.

On the drive back to Phoenix, Kate couldn't stop smiling. She wondered if she was having twins, since multiple births were often the result when fertility drugs were taken. She was going to tell Matt and her parents when she got home, but she wanted to wait until the end of her first trimester to tell everyone else. It would just be too hard to face people if she should lose the baby now. She couldn't imagine explaining that to her friends and the rest of her family.

She had contacted her doctor in Phoenix and set up an appointment for next week. She hoped Matt would be able to go with her. Suddenly, the world seemed right to her. She said a prayer that she would be able to carry the baby to term and it would be healthy, boy or girl.

The drive back to Phoenix was uneventful, but it seemed like it took forever. Kate knew it was because she was so excited to share her news with Matt. She hoped he would be as excited as she was. She also hoped that this would help them put their marriage back on track. The doctor could never pinpoint a reason for her not to get pregnant, but she wondered sometimes if Matt felt like it was his fault somehow. She was still feeling a little queasy, but she had managed to keep some crackers and ginger ale down on the drive back.

When she finally pulled into the driveway, Matt was in the garage cleaning out his truck. He smiled and waved when he saw her. He came outside and took her suitcase out of the back. "It's good to be home." Kate hoped that her face didn't give her news away, at least not yet. Matt grabbed her suitcase and followed her inside.

"I made dinner for you," Matt said excitedly. "It's your favorite, mushroom steak and potatoes."

At that moment Kate thought she was going to be ill. She put her hand over her mouth and ran to the bathroom, leaving Matt standing in the kitchen. Smells of different things were making her sick lately, even the smell of her toothpaste. This was definitely not how she had envisioned the evening.

When she came out of the bathroom, Kate sat down on the couch. Her face was pale, and her hair had come loose from her ponytail. She thought maybe that the couch was far enough from the kitchen; that the smell wouldn't bother her. Matt turned and went out to the garage. She could see the look of disappointment on his face. She had hoped for a more perfect moment than this to tell him the news, but she knew she couldn't let him think that he had let her down again.

She made her way to the garage and sat down on a stool by the wall. Matt looked up at her and asked if his cooking was always that bad. He looked like a little boy standing there, and Kate could tell it had really hurt his feelings. "Matt, thank you for making dinner; it was so thoughtful of you."

"Looks like it made you sick, not exactly the reaction I was hoping for." He reached for the car mat and gave it a shake to get the dirt out of it.

"Matt, when I was in New Mexico, I began to feel ill. I even fainted one day." Kate tried to sit very still, so she wouldn't get sick again.

"Why didn't you tell me? Do I need to take you to the doctor?" Matt suddenly looked concerned.

"No, I went to see a doctor while I was there. I thought maybe I had a virus or something. But it turns out, I'm not sick at all. I'm… pregnant. We're going to have a baby!" Matt's eyes grew wide.

"Are you sure?" Kate shook her head yes. "But I thought we had officially stopped trying." Matt looked at her with a puzzled face.

"We had, but I guess the fertility drugs must have worked a few weeks ago," Kate said with a shrug.

"I can't wait to tell everyone. They will be so excited." Matt pushed a strand of hair behind Kate's ear.

"Matt, I don't want to tell anyone other than our parents until after the first trimester. If something should happen I wouldn't want to have to explain to everyone." Kate hoped Matt understood. She had been through so much, and she just couldn't bear that.

"I understand." He softened as he kissed the top of her head gently. Matt had already thought of that too, but had not wanted to say anything. "Well, I don't feel so bad about dinner, now. Is there something I can fix you that won't make you sick?"

Kate laughed. "Maybe some soup. I made an appointment with the doctor for next Tuesday. I was hoping you could come with me."

"I wouldn't miss it." Kate took Matt's hand and they walked in the house together.

Gina had been busy at the Inn since Damian left. She had cleaned out the pantry, repotted some plants, and updated the Inn's website. Still she was having a hard time keeping him out of her thoughts. She was smiling to herself as she thought of Kate. What wonderful news! She wondered if she would be that excited to have a baby someday.

Just then the phone rang, interrupting her thoughts. "Hello, Blue Moon Inn," she answered as she tried to wash the dirt off of her hands.

"Gina?" said a man's voice on the other end.

"Yes."

"It's me, Damian. Am I interrupting something?" *Only thoughts of you.* Gina smiled to herself.

"No, I was just working in my vegetable garden. How are you?"

"I'm fine. I don't know really why I called, except that you have been on my mind lately, and I wanted to hear your voice."

Her heart melted.

"I've been thinking about you too." Gina blushed but didn't care.

"I'm having dinner with Colonel Alexander tomorrow night. He had left a message on the machine while

I was gone inviting me to dinner. He said he was going to be here for business and wanted to meet with me."

"Do you think he got the letter from your mom and that is why he wants to have dinner with you?"Gina said excitedly.

"I don't know, and he didn't say. But I was wondering the same thing." Damian began to pace.

"Are you nervous?" It was if she could see him somehow. "I know I would be." Gina rubbed some lotion on her hands as she walked around the kitchen.

"Yeah, a little. I've been trying to keep busy boxing things up around the house." *And trying not to think about you.*

"That must be really hard for you." Gina thought of him all alone in the empty house and felt sorry for him.

"It is kind of bittersweet, but it has to get done," Damian said with a sigh. They chatted a little more and Gina asked him to call after his dinner with the colonel. Damian promised he would. After they hung up, they both couldn't stop smiling. Unchartered territory was ahead for both of them. They could just feel it.

Chapter Twelve

Frank had cleaned the house from top to bottom. He even moved the stove and refrigerator and cleaned behind them. He had bought fresh flowers for the table and made sure he had all of the ingredients to fix his famous salmon. He admitted to himself that he was nervous about Maggie coming to dinner. He was glad she hadn't called to cancel, as he had worried that she would. He was afraid that after she got home and really thought about it, she might change her mind and decide not to come. But here it was, Friday afternoon, and with no word from Maggie, he assumed she would be there for dinner.

He had tried on three different shirts before deciding on one to wear. He didn't want to appear too stuffy, but yet he didn't want to look like a slob. He had taken the picture of him and Carol down and put it in a drawer. Her voice still nagged him in his mind, but it was getting less. Even work had been going well. Joyce, who sat across the hall, had teased him about being in such a good mood. She reminded him that they were at work, in case he had somehow forgotten.

Frank had bought some new cologne at the mall. He had worn the same fragrance for ten years and decided he needed a change. He had gotten a haircut, too, and had even debated about buying some hair color for men. He wasn't completely gray, but he was getting there. He decided against the hair color, mainly because he didn't know the first thing about using it, and didn't want to look ridiculous. Besides Maggie would surely notice that, and he didn't want to appear that he was trying too hard.

Frank had the salmon grilling on cedar planks, a salad made and chilling in the refrigerator, rice pilaf on the stove, and bread warming in the oven. He had even picked up a chocolate cake for dessert. He had not yet mastered baking and decided now wasn't the time to start trying to learn. Besides, he had discovered a wonderful bakery around the corner from his office, and everything tasted homemade. He checked his hair again in the mirror, and made sure he hadn't missed a spot when he shaved. He checked on the food again, and just then the doorbell rang.

Frank opened the door and there stood Maggie. She had on black pants and a cream-colored sweater, and Frank thought she had never looked better.

"Hello, come in." Frank held the door open for Maggie. "Did you have any trouble finding the place?"

"No, you gave great directions."

Maggie slipped off her jacket and handed it to Frank. She looked around the room and was surprised at how well it was decorated. She wondered if his wife had hired someone to decorate the house. It was done in deep greens and burgundy. The colors went well with the hard wood floors. She also noticed an antique cabinet in the corner, and thought it was exquisite. Frank obviously had good taste in antiques.

Maggie had taken a little extra time getting ready for their dinner date too. She was surprised at how nervous she felt. She had thought about calling earlier in the day to cancel; she was still feeling a little guilty about seeing anyone, as if she was betraying Neal in some way. She had talked to her friend, Marcie, about it, and Marcie reminded her that Neal would have wanted her to go on with her life. He never wanted her to be alone and miserable. He loved her too much to wish that for her. Maggie knew she was right, so she decided to take a chance. Frank seemed like a decent man, with a kind soul. She only hoped she was right.

Maggie handed Frank the bottle of wine she had brought. He took it into the kitchen and placed it in the ice bucket to chill. "Let me give you a tour of the house."

Frank escorted her from room to room. The house was larger than it appeared from the street, with a wonderful charm about it. He had shown her the other pieces of antique furniture he had bought, and she loved every one of them. There were quilts mixed in with modern comforters in the bedrooms, giving it a comfortable feel.

The whole house had the original hardwood flooring, which Frank explained had been refinished in the past year. The kitchen was spacious with beautiful cabinets. There was a large gas range with a copper hood, and it looked like a serious cook's kitchen.

"Have you always liked to cook?" Maggie asked as she looked around the kitchen.

"No, not really. The extent of my cooking was using the grill on the patio until after Carol left. I started watching cooking shows when I couldn't sleep, and I got hooked. I find that I really enjoy it; somehow it relaxes me and makes me feel creative."

Frank laughed, and Maggie smiled. Her blue eyes were more beautiful than he had remembered. He didn't think he would be able to refrain from kissing her tonight.

They enjoyed a wonderful meal and shared stories of their work and family. It was nice to have someone to eat with, and they truly enjoyed each other's company. Frank tried not to talk about Carol too much. In contrast, Maggie talked about Neal in almost every story she told. He could tell that she loved him very much and was still missing him. He missed Carol too, but how could you live with someone for all of those years and not miss something about them. He knew it wasn't the same. Carol had chosen to leave him; Neal did not choose to leave Maggie. He couldn't imagine ever choosing to leave a woman like her.

After dessert, they moved into the living room to continue their evening. Maggie was surprised at how comfortable the leather couch was. She was feeling more relaxed. *Probably from the wine*, she thought. "You have a lovely home." Maggie sighed as she rested her head on the back of the sofa.

"Thank you. I really like it. From the day I found it, I knew this was the place for me."

"I take it Carol didn't agree," Maggie asked cautiously.

"Carol wanted different things. She liked a more modern look, and apparently a more modern man." Frank frowned as he said it.

He suddenly realized that no matter how he tried, he could never have been the kind of man Carol wanted. He was down to earth and predictable, like the antiques he had. Carol had tried her best to mold him into what she wanted and when she realized she couldn't, she decided to move on. She wanted flash and excitement, and he was stable and boring. He wondered if she had found her Mr. Excitement yet.

"Carol did some of the decorating," Frank said, trying to give her a little credit. "I made some changes after she left and added the antiques."

"I love the antique furniture. The pieces are precisely what I would have chosen myself. I have thought about doing some redecorating, but it's hard to change things." Maggie looked sad as she said it. Frank had the feeling that she was referring to more than just furniture.

"Change is difficult, but it can be liberating at the same time." Frank reached for her hand.

"I guess that is true. I've told myself I wasn't changing anything because it might upset Elizabeth. But the truth is that I'm afraid if I change anything, then the memories will begin to fade. If I lose the memories, then I am losing all that I have left of Neal. It makes me feel disloyal somehow." Maggie surprised herself at how open and honest she was with Frank.

"I can't say that I know how you feel because divorce and death are two different things. But I do know that clinging to memories will not bring the person back. No one can ever take your memories from you, and even if you moved far away, those memories would go with you." He squeezed her hand.

"You are a very wise man." Maggie smiled but the sadness still shone in her eyes. They sat that way for a long time, just sipping wine and looking at the fire. Frank knew that if he wanted to win Maggie's heart, he was going to have to take things slowly. He didn't want to rush her and scare her away. After all that she had been through, she needed someone to care for her and to love her again.

After a while Maggie decided it was time she drove home. It was an hour away and she didn't want to get home too late. Frank invited her to dinner and a movie the next weekend. He was going to drive to her place this time. "I'd offer to make you dinner, but I'm afraid I don't cook nearly as well as you do," Maggie said with a little laugh.

"No need to cook, I'll take you out. You decide where you would like to go and I will pick you up at five on Saturday."

"I'd like that very much." Maggie reached up to hug Frank and she kissed him on the cheek. "I had a nice evening. The food was delicious and the company even better. Thank you." Frank kissed her hand and walked her to her car.

"I'm glad to see you have the top up tonight."

"It would be a little chilly, I'm afraid, to have it down after dark."

Frank watched as Maggie pulled out of the driveway. It had taken all of his will not to grab her and kiss her. But he knew she was testing the waters, and that he needed to go slow. He didn't mind. She was well worth the wait.

Chapter Thirteen

Damian was nervous as he drove to Rogers for dinner. He had worn khaki pants and a polo shirt. He wondered what the colonel would look like out of uniform. He parked and went inside and could see Colonel Alexander already waiting for him at a table in the corner. "Hello, sir." Damian shook the colonel's hand before sitting down across from him.

"We aren't at work, so please, call me Dave." Damian swallowed hard. It was going to be strange to call him Dave, but he would try. He had on dress pants and a cotton shirt, and he looked younger than he did in his uniform. Damian was studying him, trying to determine if they looked alike in some way. They had the same eye color; he had already determined that. They were a steely blue that deepened if the light was right.

"So, how have you been, Damian? I know it must be difficult for you to be back here since your mother passed away." Dave leaned back in his chair.

"Yes, sir, it has. I've been busy trying to sort through everything and box up the things I want to keep. I'm considering selling the house." Damian felt a knot in his stomach.

"Don't make serious decisions too hastily; grief has a way of clouding your thinking." He was speaking from experience.

Damian took a drink of water and the waitress came to take their order. Colonel Alexander looked at Damian and smiled. After looking at his face, Damian knew. There in his face were the same dimples he saw every day in the mirror. "Did you read the letter from your mother yet?" The colonel fidgeted with his napkin.

"Yes, I did, finally, just a few days ago, in fact."

The colonel didn't know how else to go about it, so he decided to handle it in a straightforward manner, the way it had everything else in his life. There was no point in beating around the bush. So he took a deep breath and said, "I received one from her too. Apparently the attorney mailed them at the same time. I read it the day I received it. It appears that I am your father." They sat looking at each other for a long moment, neither of them sure of how the other would react.

"Then it is you! After I read the letter from my mother, I thought you had to be my father. I couldn't believe that fate had allowed us to serve together in the Corps. I respect you immensely, and I am just as shocked by this as you must be, sir," Damian said.

"I will always be grateful to your mother. She is what helped me stay alive all the time I was in the POW camp in 'Nam. I loved her with every ounce of my being, and I don't think I ever quite got over her. I was devastated to learn she had married and had a child once I returned to the States. I couldn't blame her; she thought I had died. She had waited as long as she could and then had to move on with her life. But when I found out that we had a child, I actually sat down and cried. I was so overjoyed, and to realize that you were right there with me, it was if God had put us together at last. You are the kind of person I would have chosen for a son, but even better, you really are my son." The colonel smiled from ear to ear, but had to wipe away a tear from his eye. Damian couldn't believe that the colonel actually cried. It made him see the human side of him, and he respected him even more for allowing him to see it.

"Why didn't you say something to me sooner?" Damian took another drink of water. He was finding it difficult not to cry himself.

"For one thing, I was fairly certain you had not read the letter from your mother. The other reason is that I wouldn't have been allowed to be your command-ing officer if the Corps had found out you were my son. I know it is against the rules, but I really wanted the chance to get to know you better. It allowed me to spend time with you, and for that I am grateful."

"You know, even though you are my biological father, I had a wonderful man for a dad." Damian felt he had to defend him somehow. Dave shifted in his seat; he knew this was coming.

"I'm very glad you had a dad. I don't know what kind of one I would have made. I don't get to see my daughter very often because I'm so busy with the Marine Corps. And when I do see her, I don't really know what to say to her. She just kind of grew up when I wasn't looking." He smiled, and there were those dimples again.

"Does your daughter know about me?" Damian felt strange knowing he had a sister.

"Not yet, but I will tell her. I think you would like her if you met her. Her name is Tessa." Dave took out his wallet and showed Damian a picture of her. She was nice looking and had long dark hair. It seemed odd to think that he was no longer an only child.

"I would like to meet her if she is willing." Damian wondered how she would feel about that.

"She always wanted a brother or a sister. Her mother and I divorced before we could make that happen. She goes to college on the East Coast near her mother. She will be coming for a visit for spring break, and maybe we could get together then."

"I'd like that." Damian returned the smile and the dimples that came along with it.

Just then their food arrived, and they were glad for the distraction. So much information had been shared in just a few minutes. It was a lot to absorb. Damian was already thinking of Gina and how excited she would be to hear the news.

After dinner they talked about the Corps. Colonel Alexander was going to be taking over a command post at Twentynine Palms in California. Damian told him he was reporting to Camp Pendleton near San Diego, and the colonel said he already knew. They were only going to be stationed a few hours away from each other, and both were grateful for the chance to spend some time together. The colonel told Damian that he planned to retire soon, which didn't come as a surprise Damian.

"Sir, I know you asked me to call you Dave. It seems a little strange to me. I know you are my father, but I already had a dad. I'm just not sure what to call you." He felt he had to be honest with him.

"You'll figure out what fits as time goes on. I don't care what you call me, as long as you call me. I've missed out on too much already, and I don't want to waste the time we have left to get to know each other and be a family. I'm grateful to your mother for finally telling us the truth. She was a wonderful woman, and I hope you won't be angry with her."

"To tell you the truth, I was very angry at her when I first read the letter. But after I thought about it and thought about her, I began to understand. I know things were very different when she was younger, and I'm sure she did what she thought was best for everyone involved." Damian finished the last bite of his potatoes.

"I'm sure she wondered what kind of father I could have been because the Corps would come first. She knew that about me and loved me anyway. She was a special woman. If you ever find a woman that can tolerate the Corps and love you anyway, then marry her." Dave smiled, but his words had a twinge of regret in them.

"Is that what happened with your wife?" Damian hoped he wasn't getting too personal.

"She tolerated the Corps in the beginning. But after a few deployments and nights where I didn't come home because we were out on operations, she had enough. Said she felt like a single parent, and in many ways she was. She enjoyed the social part of being an officer's wife, but she wasn't willing to make the sacrifices that go with it." He sounded sad and Damian wondered if he regretted putting the Corps before her.

"She has remarried and moved on with her life. He is a dentist, so very stable and home every night. I can't imagine leading such a boring life myself."

Damian laughed at the colonel and had the answer to his question. He knew exactly what he meant. He couldn't imagine an office job. He would have been bored to tears. Once you had been in the Corps nothing else would do. It kind of got into your blood somehow, and he knew it was the place for him, just as his father did. He only hoped someday he could find a woman who would love him enough to tolerate it. An image of Gina flashed through his mind. He tried to imagine his life with her, and wondered if she would ever be able to be happy living the life of a military wife.

Damian and his father talked for another two hours. They talked about the Marine Corps and about Damian's mother. He was fascinated at the stories Dave told about his mom. He had not known she was an excellent dancer and had been very beautiful when she was younger. He could tell that he had been very much in love with her. His stories of his many adventures in the Marine Corps were entertaining. Damian told him he should write a book about his many years in the Corps. Dave told him he had thought about it after he retired. He told him the good along with the bad, and it made Damian respect him even more for his honesty. He asked Damian many questions about his life. It was as if they were trying to fit a lifetime into just a few hours.

Finally, Dave paid the check, and they were standing in the parking lot. Neither of them knew what to say. They promised each other they would be in touch soon and planned on getting together once they both were stationed in California. Damian reached out his hand for a handshake, and his father surprised him by grabbing him and hugging him tightly.

"I'm very proud of you, Damian. Your parents did a fine job raising you. I deeply regret that I didn't get to know you sooner, but now that you are in my life, I'll be damned if I'm going to ever let you go."

Damian swallowed to hold back the tears. Finally, he choked out, "I'm proud to be your son." They hugged once more and then got into their cars. Damian watched as his father drove out of sight.

It had been an incredible evening. Damian thought back on all his father had said. He was an amazing man, and he could see why his mother had loved him. He felt blessed to be given this chance to get to know him. He only wished his mother was still alive so she could have gotten to know him again. It was clear that he still carried a torch for her. Suddenly, he didn't feel so alone in the world anymore. He had a father and a sister, and he hoped she would welcome him into her family too.

Damian pulled into the garage and made his way into the house. He flipped on the lights and walked between the boxes in the hallway. As he sat on the couch, he dialed Gina's number. He knew it was late, but somehow he knew she would be waiting to hear from him.

After the third ring, Damian started to hang up the phone, but then Gina answered.

"I'm sorry to call so late, did I wake you?" Damian was apologetic.

"No, not at all. I was just mixing up some dough for some cinnamon rolls in the morning. That is why I didn't answer sooner; I was trying to get the dough off of my hands." Gina dried her hands on the tea towel in the kitchen.

"Well, I had dinner with the colonel tonight." Damian paused.

"And?" Gina couldn't stand the suspense.

"He is my father." The words sounded strange as he said them. It was going to take some time to get used to the idea of being related to the colonel.

"Oh, Damian! How do you feel about that?" Gina made her way to a stool in the kitchen. She needed to sit down for this, she decided.

"Really good, actually. We had a long talk, and I learned things about my mom I never knew. I could tell he had really loved her. We talked about the Marine Corps, and I found out he is going to be stationed just a few hours from me in California." Damian had already been thinking of some things they could do together.

"That is great. I take it you two plan on spending some time together."

"Definitely. He gave me a big hug when I left." Damian was surprised at how easy it was to be so open with Gina.

"I'm so happy that things worked out. I know he will never replace your dad, but it is wonderful that you two can finally have a relationship." Gina smiled. She couldn't imagine a better outcome for him.

"I respect him very much. The only thing is I don't know exactly what to call him. He told me I could call him Dave, but that seems a little strange," Damian admitted.

"Why not just call him Dave for now and see what happens? In time, you might want to call him Dad or Pop. That is what I call my Dad sometimes," Gina suggested.

"Yeah, maybe," Damian said, but couldn't imagine ever calling him anything but colonel.

Damian told Gina more about the evening with his father. She was such a good listener, but he felt a little guilty for taking up so much of her time. He asked her about how things were going at the Inn.

"Just fine." *It isn't the same without you here,* she thought, but didn't say it.

"I hope you don't mind if I call you," Damian squirmed a little as he said it. What would he do if she did mind? He would be crushed.

"I don't mind at all. As a matter of fact, if you hadn't called me by tomorrow evening, I was going to call you. The suspense was killing me!" Damian laughed as he thought of Gina pacing the floor wondering how his evening went.

"I really meant it when I said I was going to stop by and see you on my way to California." Damian hoped she still thought that was a good idea.

"Why don't you come early and stay a few days at the Inn? It will be my treat." Gina couldn't believe she had just invited Damian to come stay with her. She hoped that wasn't too forward.

"Wow, that would be great. But I can pay for a room. I would be taking up a paying customer's room, and I wouldn't want to put you out."

He's considerate, Gina thought. "Nonsense! It is a slower time of year and I'm not completely booked for another month. Besides, I'd love your company." Gina was blushing again. She couldn't believe what she had just said, but it slipped out before she thought about it. Funny how the truth just came tumbling out, when she didn't plan on it.

"Then I will be there in a couple of weeks. That should give me plenty of time to finish packing up here. Is it okay if I call you in the meantime?" He knew the answer to that, but wanted to make sure.

"Of course. Call me anytime you'd like." *Like twice a day,* she was thinking. She could picture him smiling and his dimples.

"Thanks, Gina. You've been a great friend through all of this. I don't know what I would have done without you." Damian was thinking of her sitting in the kitchen with her long legs and beautiful green eyes.

"You're welcome. Now get some sleep. Goodnight." Damian sat on the couch and couldn't help smiling to himself. Little did he know that Gina was doing the same thing in New Mexico.

Chapter Fourteen

Kate was trying to take her nausea as a good sign. It wasn't exactly morning sickness; it came and went all day. Surely this must be a sign that her hormones were doing what they were supposed to do, so she tried to console herself with that. Matt had taken to eating foods that didn't have much of an aroma, so as not make Kate feel worse. He had been very sweet to her since she got home; she had a feeling he had missed her. She had gone back to work at the bank, but it was hard to concentrate when she felt sick off and on during the day. She hoped no one questioned her about it. She just wasn't ready to share the good news yet.

When Kate came home from work Matt had a bouquet of flowers on the table. He was in the kitchen fixing some soup and a sandwich.

"Hi there," he said as he put the bread away. "Feel like eating a little something?" He put two plates on the table and went to stir the soup.

"I think I could eat a bowl of soup and if that goes well, I might attempt a sandwich." Kate smiled wearily. She was so tired lately, she hoped that was normal during pregnancy and not a sign something was wrong. She had a doctor's appointment in the morning and she was anxious to talk to her regular doctor.

"The flowers are beautiful." Kate bent to smell the bouquet. Tulips were one of her favorites, and she was touched that Matt had remembered.

"I stopped by Posies on my way home from work. You might be interested to know that the shop is for sale." Matt watched Kate for her reaction.

"Are you serious?" Kate's eyes grew wide. She already knew what he was thinking.

"I know we talked about it before, but do you really think that now is the time for me to quit my job and take on a business venture?" Her voice was rising as she said it.

"Calm down. It was just an idea. I thought if you owned your own flower shop then it would be easier for you once the baby came. You could take it with you to work for a few hours a day or even have a sitter at the shop, so you could nurse the baby. They already have a couple of people that work there, so you wouldn't have to run things all by yourself. Think about it. It would be a lot less stressful than working at the bank." Matt tried to be reasonable, but the look on her face told him she didn't agree.

"I'll think about it, but I really don't think now is the time," Kate said matter-of-factly.

"I think now is the perfect time." Matt put a bowl of soup in front of Kate. He couldn't believe that she would pass up such an opportunity, a dream really, just because she was pregnant.

"Kate, you have to consider that the baby won't be a baby forever. He or she will go to school and grow up. Owning the flower shop would give you a lot of freedom, plus you would be doing something you love to do. I know it is work too, but at least you wouldn't have to answer to anyone except yourself." Matt was trying to help her see the bigger picture.

"And don't forget the bank. We would have to take out a loan to buy the shop, and I would have to make a profit in order to stay in business. With the added expenses a baby will bring to our lives, I just don't see that this is the right time for this." Kate was the one with the business degree; she felt Matt should listen to her.

"The shop has to be profitable, and if it isn't you are the perfect person to turn it around. With your business sense and your passion for flowers, how can you go wrong? Besides, can you really see yourself working at the bank for the next twenty years? I know it's a good job, but for once in your life don't play it safe. Risk a little. You will regret it later if you don't at least try." Matt couldn't believe she wouldn't be more open-minded about this. He expected her to be excited about the idea, but again he was wrong.

Kate told Matt she would think about it, but not to get his hopes up too much. Matt had already decided that he would look into purchasing the shop a little further. He wanted more for Kate than she wanted for herself; he only wished she could see that. He was tired of arguing with her. He was beginning to think that maybe they really did want very different things out of life.

Kate was up before the alarm rang. She hadn't slept well because she was anxious about her doctor's appointment. Dr. Yang had been wonderful through all of her fertility issues and in vitro attempts. She knew she was going to be surprised that she was pregnant. Kate really needed to have her reassurance that everything was progressing well. She also hoped the doctor could give her something to combat the daily nausea.

Kate was sitting on the edge of the bed nibbling a cracker when Matt got up and went in the bathroom to shower. After their conversation about the flower shop, he hadn't said much to Kate. She knew he was upset by her reaction, but she thought he was being unreasonable. How could she focus on a business when she was so worried about the pregnancy? The additional stress of starting a business couldn't be good for the baby she reasoned.

Kate managed to keep the cracker down, and went into the kitchen to start the coffee. She wasn't drinking much of it herself lately, but she knew Matt would want a few cups before they left for her appointment. She dressed and was putting on her makeup when Matt got out of the shower. "I'm sorry if I upset you last night." Matt wrapped a towel around his waist.

"I guess the idea of my own business is scary to me. It is also stressful, which I don't think is good for the baby."

"Kate, you are not going to be pregnant forever. You are treating this like something permanent, but you will deliver the baby in about eight or nine months and then what? You aren't thinking long term. And I don't see how running your own business is any more stressful than what you deal with on a day to day basis at the bank." Matt wasn't going to let this issue drop. It was just too important.

"The difference is if I fail, then we will be ruined financially. How can we plan for college if the business fails?" Kate frowned as she pinned her hair back.

"Why do you have to be so pessimistic? What if the business thrives, and we have college money set aside by the time the kid is ten years old? Besides, we have some money in the bank. We can take out a home equity loan or borrow the money from my parents if we need to. I'm making a good salary, we could squeak by on that for a while until you got things going." *Matt always saw the glass as half full*, Kate thought.

"Can we discuss this later, please? I'm a little nervous about my doctor's appointment, and I don't need any more stress right now." Kate turned and walked out of the bathroom.

Dr. Yang was surprised when Kate told her the news of her pregnancy. She wanted to run some additional tests to make sure her HCG levels were where they needed to be. By her best calculation Kate was about seven weeks pregnant. "It is too soon to hear the baby's heartbeat, but we should be able to at your next appointment." Dr. Yang wrote out a prescription for some medication to help with the nausea. Kate had lost about five pounds, and Dr. Yang said that wasn't uncommon. She told her not to worry that she would gain that back and more. She told her to take her prenatal vitamins and did a brief exam. Kate was relieved that everything seemed to be just fine.

Matt sat through most of the appointment without saying much. Dr. Yang asked if either of them had any questions. Kate was surprised when Matt spoke up. "Dr. Yang, would it cause undue stress to the baby if Kate were to quit her current job and buy a flower shop and take over as owner there?" Kate's jaw dropped open as she turned to look at Matt. She gave him a look that told him he had crossed the line. Dr. Yang could sense this was more than just a hypothetical question from looking at them.

"Well, many women continue to work during their pregnancies, and many women have stressful jobs. They often have to juggle not only a job and a pregnancy, but often additional children at home or ailing parents too. As long as the job doesn't pose any health risks, like being exposed to measles, per se, then I don't think that it would be harmful to the baby." Dr. Yang smiled and patted Kate's hand. "I know it has been a long road to get to this point. I know how much you want this baby and how long you've waited, but you can't live in a box for nine months, and I wouldn't recommend it if you could. Eat well, get plenty of rest, and be reasonable about activity. Other than that, enjoy this time. There will never be another time in your life when it will be just the two of you." Dr. Yang told Kate to call if she had any questions, and that she should schedule another appointment in four weeks.

Kate and Matt walked to the car in silence. She couldn't believe he had asked Dr. Yang about the flower shop. She thought he was way out of line, and that it wasn't his decision anyway. Maybe being pregnant was not going to put their marriage back on track after all. Maybe it was going to be what ultimately drove them apart.

As they were driving home, Matt reached over and took Kate's hand and gave it a squeeze. "See, everything is going fine. No need to worry." He smiled and signaled his next turn.

"If you think your little stunt in Dr. Yang's office was your way of making me buy the flower shop, then you don't know me very well. I can't believe you did that!" Kate tried to keep her voice even as she looked out the window.

"I knew you were never going to ask. You would just use the stress issue as an excuse not to buy the flower shop. Now, you can't hide behind that anymore." Matt's patience was growing thin. He moved his hand back to the steering wheel.

"Is that what you think, that I'm hiding?" Kate felt tears sting her eyes.

"Kate, you have always been one to play it safe, even if that meant sacrificing your happiness. You went into business because you thought there were more job opportunities even though you really wanted to do something else. You worry about money, yet you are the most frugal person I know. You won't even spend more than eight dollars for a bottle of wine!" Kate was crying now, and there was just no stopping it. "Can't you see that I want you to be happy? For us to be happy? I know running a flower shop of your own would make you happy. We might have to live on a little less, but I am more than willing to do that. Life is too short to be miserable." Matt pulled into the driveway, got out of the car and slammed the door. If she wanted to work at a bank until she was seventy, then why should he care? He was beginning to wonder if their marriage was in serious trouble.

Kate drove herself to work. She didn't see the point in taking the whole day off, when her doctor's appointment only took up the morning. Besides, she hated the thought of work piling up on her desk when she wasn't there. She also knew she needed a distraction from the argument she had with Matt. She couldn't believe he was pushing this issue. The more she thought about the things he said, the more she knew he was right.

She always played it safe. She had always been the des-
ignated driver because she didn't trust anyone else to
stay sober. She studied for exams a week in advance
because she was afraid of not being prepared. She had
extras of everything around the house so they wouldn't
run out of anything. How had she gotten to this point?
Was this going to be the final straw that would drive a
permanent wedge between her and her husband?

On her way home from work she decided to stop
by and see her parents. She had already told them the
news of the baby, and asked them to keep it quiet until
she was through her first trimester. She needed an
objective opinion, and knew she could count on her
Dad to give her one.

When she got to her parents' house, they were in
the family room watching the news on TV.

"Hey, there's my girl. How are you?"

Her Dad got up from the recliner to give her a hug.
Her mom was crocheting something as she sat on the
couch. Her parents could tell by looking at her that
something was troubling her. She had always worn
her heart on her sleeve ever since she was a little girl.
She explained to her parents the idea Matt had about
them buying the flower shop. She was trying not to
interject her opinion before seeing what they thought
of the idea.

"Well, I think you should run the numbers and see
before you decide one way or the other. You've got a
good business sense, and you will be able to tell if it is
something that could be profitable or not. But equally

important, you should consider what you would like to do, not just what you think you should do. I know how much you love working with plants and flowers. I think that would be a good fit for you. You don't always have to play it safe." Her Dad smiled and put an arm around her shoulders. Kate wondered if he had been talking to Matt.

"But how will I manage that with a baby?" Kate sighed. Kate's mother spoke up.

"I think you would have the opportunity to spend more time with the baby if you were your own boss, than if you worked for someone else. You could even have the baby at the shop sometimes, which would make it easier to nurse." Her mother sounded a lot like Matt. Kate hugged them both and thanked them for the advice. Maybe she had been too closed minded about the idea. Her mother asked her if she wanted to stay for dinner, but Kate said she was tired and would call them later in the week.

She decided on the drive home that she would at least look into buying the flower shop further, maybe it would turn out to be a bad deal after all, and Matt would leave her alone about it. She was so tired. She would be glad when the first trimester was over. She stopped by the drug store to pick up the prescription Dr. Yang had given her. She hoped it helped the nausea, because it was getting almost unbearable.

When she got home, Matt was nowhere to be found. She found a note on the table saying he went to shoot some hoops and would be back later, not to wait up. She figured he needed to blow off some steam. She also knew he would probably have a beer or two with his friends before heading home. She was glad for the peace and quiet. She fixed herself some toast and tea and then went in to take a long hot bath. She was surprised when she woke up in a tub of cold water and Matt was calling her name. She must have fallen asleep, but she couldn't believe she had slept that long in the tub.

She decided to wait to talk to Matt about the flower shop. She was just too drained to argue about it. Matt seemed in a better mood and went into the kitchen to fix a snack. When he came back into the bedroom, she was fast asleep. At least she was in bed this time. He hoped the entire pregnancy would not be like this. He loved Kate, but the stress of trying to conceive and now the realities of expecting a baby were more than he bargained for.

Chapter Fifteen

Frank had done nothing but think about Maggie since their dinner date. The more time he spent with her the more he liked her, he only hoped she felt the same. He was looking forward to their dinner and movie date and had bought a new shirt for the occasion. He could hear Carol saying he was worse than a woman, but it was getting easier to quiet her voice in his head. He had called Maggie in the middle of the week just to see how she was doing. She was touched by the gesture, he could tell. He was picking her up at five, and then they were going to have dinner at an Italian restaurant before heading to the movie. Maggie said she would take care of the reservations.

Maggie had thought more about Frank than she cared to admit. Every time she thought about him, she felt a twinge of guilt for not thinking about Neal. She knew she was going to have to move past this in order to get on with her life. She also knew that she was going to have to stop comparing them to each other. There were some qualities about Frank that were different from Neal, and she hated to admit it, but some of them she preferred. She liked his love of antiques and how he decorated his house. She liked that he was organized and neat. Neither she nor Neal had been either of those things, and although it made for spontaneity, it often made for poor planning. Many times they had taken a trip on a whim and ended up in a flea bag motel or sleeping in the car because they didn't bother making reservations in advance.

Neal hadn't planned much for his retirement either. She was grateful that they had taken out a life insurance policy after Elizabeth was born. At least she was able to live comfortably for now if she watched her finances and didn't run up the credit cards again. She had a passion for shopping, and was trying her best to channel that passion into a new direction. Neal had enjoyed shopping almost as much as she had, and they bought new furniture every few years for their house. She wished now that they had invested that money instead.

Maggie had been writing more since she returned from the Blue Moon Inn. Elizabeth would be home from college in a couple of weeks for spring break, and she was looking forward to that. Even though she knew she would be busy with her friends, it was comforting to have her sleeping back in her room again.

Maggie was proud of herself because she had already made reservations for dinner at the Italian restaurant.

She was trying to be more organized. She had cleaned the house and gone through some things in the garage. She knew she needed to go through Neal's things, but she just wasn't quite ready for that.

Maggie took some extra time dressing for her date with Frank. She thought he had been a perfect gentleman so far, but she wondered if he would at least kiss her this time. The thought of kissing someone other than Neal frightened her a little. It had been so long, would it all come back to her? She decided on a black cashmere sweater with a small strand of pearls. It was elegant but not flashy. She had gone to the salon and gotten her hair highlighted and nails done. She hadn't pampered herself so much for months, and it felt good. She wasn't dead yet, she reminded herself, she was still amongst the living and she needed to start acting like it.

Frank had pressed his new shirt and changed pants twice before deciding which pair to wear. He had polished his shoes and taken an extra long time shaving. He splashed on some of his new cologne and headed to the car. He had even cleaned and washed his car for the occasion. He stopped by the flower shop on his way and bought roses for Maggie. He wasn't sure which color was her favorite, so he got one in red, yellow, pink and white. It amazed him that no matter how old he got, it still made him nervous to go out with a woman. But, he decided, it also made him feel young and alive, and he had been missing that for far too long.

Frank was surprised when he arrived at Maggie's house. He had expected it to be large and modern, but it wasn't. It was more like a cottage, with stone on the front and a wrought iron gate that opened to the sidewalk. He rang the bell and waited. After a few moments, Maggie appeared at the door. When she saw the roses, her face lit up. She hadn't received flowers for so long. Frank explained that he wasn't sure what color was her favorite, so he had gotten one of each. Maggie laughed at him, and then took the flowers and put them in a vase with some water.

Maggie gave Frank a quick tour of her house. The furniture was more modern than his, but not extreme. There were pictures of family everywhere. Frank thought that the man and girl in most of the pictures must be Neal and Elizabeth. If so, they were both very attractive people. The kitchen was recently remodeled and had a breakfast nook. Maggie's office was the only room that was not neat and tidy. There were papers everywhere and books stacked on the floor. She apologized for the way it looked, but said if she moved anything then she couldn't find it. It was an odd sort of organization, but it worked for her.

Frank and Maggie had a wonderful time at dinner, and Frank drove this time. Maggie had a way of making Frank feel totally at ease, and he liked that about her. He loved the way her face lit up when she laughed. They talked about some of Maggie's travels and about her family. She had grown up on a farm in the Midwest, and had some very interesting tales. Frank noticed that she hadn't mentioned Neal at all, and wondered if she was making an effort not to talk about him.

On the way to the car, Frank held Maggie's hand. She couldn't believe his touch made her stomach do a little flip, but it did. They went to a movie, a romantic comedy they both had wanted to see, and enjoyed it very much. It was the perfect date movie. Frank put his arm around Maggie during the movie and left it there the entire time. It made her feel safe and protected, and she liked that.

Frank was sorry to see the evening end. He asked Maggie if she wanted to go for ice cream, but she declined. She said she was still full from dinner. She invited him in for a glass of wine, which sounded better to him anyway. As they were chatting, the phone rang and Maggie excused herself to answer it. Frank could tell by her end of the conversation that it must be Elizabeth. Finally Maggie returned and apologized. "Elizabeth and her boyfriend have had an argument and she is very upset. I told her I would call her back." Maggie looked apologetically at Frank. "I'm terribly sorry." Maggie took Frank's hand.

"It's fine. I need to head back anyway, and it is getting late."

Frank squeezed Maggie's hand and forced a smile. He had to admire her for being such a good mother. "Would it be all right if I called you this week? I was thinking maybe we could go on a picnic or something next week." Frank sounded hopeful.

"I would love that! Again, I'm sorry, Frank. I've had a wonderful evening. Thank you." Maggie reached up to kiss Frank on the cheek. She lingered for a few seconds, and then she could feel Frank kissing her. It was warm and tender, and she was feeling heat rise to her cheeks. She didn't want it to end. Suddenly it all came back to her, and she had to fight to push images of Neal out of her mind. Frank sensed something had changed, and pulled back. He smiled awkwardly and said he would let himself out.

Maggie sat on the couch after Frank left. *Why is this so hard,* she wondered? She had really enjoyed kissing Frank and didn't understand why she kept thinking of Neal. She felt guilty, as if she were cheating on Neal. She knew that was absurd, but that is how she felt. She sighed and picked up the phone to call Elizabeth. She wanted to be there for her daughter, but found she was having a hard time concentrating on their conversation. Maggie told Elizabeth she would call her tomorrow to check on her. She felt spent and wondered if she would ever be able to fall in love again.

Chapter Sixteen

Damian had managed to go through all of the rooms in the house and pack up what he wanted to put in storage. He had called a local church that took donations and had donated some things, including a few pieces of furniture. Somehow, he knew his mother would have been proud of him for that. The rest of the things he took to a storage unit. There was a small amount of furniture still left in the house, including his bed. He had contacted a realtor to come over and list the house, so that was taken care of. He was surprised when the realtor told him what he thought the house was worth. Damian decided he would set that money aside in case he ever did get married, once the house sold. The thought of a big wedding without his parents there depressed him a little. He knew the colonel would be there, but it wouldn't be quite the same. He shook his head to clear his thoughts. Why was he thinking about his wedding? He didn't even have a girlfriend.

Damian had called Gina several times in the past two weeks, and each time they had talked for more than an hour. He discovered they liked the same music and had many things in common. He was excited about getting to see her before he reported to his next duty station. He knew a couple of the guys from his previous unit were also being stationed at Camp Pendleton, so he would know someone there at least. Gina had given him some ideas of things to see and do in the area. He only wished that she would join him.

The night before he was leaving to go west, he called his friend, Greg, to see if he wanted to have dinner. He had seen him a couple of times since he had been back, and it was fun to hang out with him again. Greg was one of those people that never seemed to change, but somehow Damian found that comforting.

They had dinner at a burger place near Greg's house. Damian decided to tell Greg about Gina. He wasn't going to tell him about his real father and all that he had discovered since reading his mom's letter. He knew it was something his mom would not have wanted people to know about, even now.

"Boy, you've got it bad," Greg teased Damian as they finished their dinner.

"What are you talking about?" Damian wiped sauce off of his chin.

"I can tell by the look in your eyes that you are really falling for Gina. She must be something special for you to step back from the Corps long enough to look." Greg knew Damian could have had about any woman he wanted, but Damian had never been that kind of guy. He was too decent and caring to use a woman, and Greg respected him for that.

"There is just something about her. I don't know exactly what it is, really. She listens to me, and she makes me feel good about myself. She doesn't judge. Of course, she has gorgeous green eyes and long beautiful legs, which doesn't hurt either." They both laughed at his description. "I just don't know if it is fair to get involved with her, when we will be living so far apart. Even if we did get serious, I'm not sure she is the kind of woman that would understand the Marine Corps life. You know how my life is with deployments, being gone for months at a time, being called at a moment's notice to go fight a war on the other side of the world. It is a lot to ask of a woman to tolerate that." Damian knew that having a wife and maybe kids at home would make missions more difficult. He had seen too many of his friends get Dear John letters from wives and girlfriends back home.

"Why don't you give it a chance and see where it goes? It would be her decision, and I think she is smart enough to know what she is getting into." Greg tried to reassure him, but was not sure if he was convincing. Greg dropped Damian back off at his house in his old blue car. They hugged good-bye, and Damian promised to keep in touch.

"Let me know when you finally decide to get a different car," Damian shouted as he got out.

Never! I told you this is going to be a classic," Greg shot back, smiling.

Damian unlocked the door to the house. It felt so empty and dark. He could hardly believe that this would be his last night to ever sleep here again. But he knew that all of the memories he had he would carry in his heart; he didn't need a building to remind him of anything. Somehow he sensed his mother would be happy with the choices he'd made. Not just about the house but about his father. Damian felt peaceful as he packed the last few things he needed before leaving for New Mexico and then on to California.

Gina was so excited that Damian was coming she could hardly stand it. Vivian had been giving her a hard time for two weeks, but deep down she hoped things worked out for them. Gina deserved a guy like Damian, and, as much as Gina loved running the Inn, Vivian didn't want her to turn into an old lady in the desert alone.

Gina had asked Vivian if she could work a few extra hours while Damian was there so they could spend some time together. She wanted to take him for a picnic on the mesa and to the art galleries downtown. More than anything, she just wanted to get to know him better. Their long conversations had been wonderful, and the more she knew him the more she liked him. Every time she thought about his smile it made her heart melt. She didn't know where this was headed, but she was trying to keep her heart in check. She didn't know if she would be able to live the life of a Marine wife, if it ever got that serious. She was trying not to think about it too much, because she wanted to give Damian a chance.

Gina was glad this was a slow time of year at the Inn. With a little advance planning, she had been able to prepare some of the food for the meals and put it in the freezer, so Vivian wouldn't have much to do in her absence. She had chosen a different room for Damian to stay in, one on the end that had the nicest views, she thought. She had been spending more time in her garden and had a nice golden tan. She was so excited she hardly slept at all and was up early the next morning, eager for Damian to arrive.

As Gina finished her cup of tea, the phone rang. She was surprised to hear Kate West's voice.

"Gina," Kate began, "I'm sorry to bother you, is this a bad time?" Kate asked politely.

"No, not at all. Is everything all right?" Gina was worried there was a problem with the baby.

"Everything is going fine. I had a good check-up with my doctor, and Matt is excited about the baby. I actually was calling to ask your opinion about a business matter." Kate twirled her hair absentmindedly as she talked to Gina.

"Well, I'm honored that you would want my opinion." Gina couldn't imagine what advice she could want from her.

"I think I told you when I was there about how much I liked flowers and gardening. I have an opportunity to buy a flower shop. But I am really scared. I've never run my own business before and taking on something new like this now that I'm pregnant seems even scarier. I wanted to know what you thought. You've been running a business, what do you like and dislike about it?"

Gina thought for a moment before answering, "What I like most about it is the freedom. I can control my own schedule, and I don't have a boss to answer to every day. I also love meeting new people, so that is a plus for me. The downside, I suppose, if there is one, is that the days can be a little long sometimes. And for me, I don't ever get to leave work so to speak, because I live here. You wouldn't have that problem with a flower shop." Kate laughed. "I think that if you like what you're doing, and can stand a little risk, then it sounds like a fabulous opportunity. You could even take the baby to work with you part of the time. And if you have any employees who can manage things, it would make it much easier to take off work if you or the baby were sick," Gina offered. Kate hadn't thought about that before. She knew what a hassle it was at the bank to cover for someone else when they called in sick, and she tried to limit her absences as much as possible. Kate and Gina talked for a few more minutes. Gina asked her to be sure and let her know what she decided, and Kate promised she would.

Kate felt better after talking to Gina. She thought about the peaceful garden at the Inn and found herself missing it. Maybe if she worked around flowers and plants all the time, she would feel peaceful. Maybe it was her calling. Kate decided to stop by the flower shop on her lunch break and talk with the owner. She would ask to see the balance sheets and decide if it was a good financial risk. Other than a little nausea, she felt good. She felt more confident than she had in a long time. She decided that maybe she would give business ownership a chance. After all, if she failed, she could always go back to banking she reasoned. But she knew that an opportunity like this didn't come along every day, so she needed to make up her mind.

Gina hurried around the kitchen to prepare breakfast for the guests. There were three rooms occupied, but she figured only part of the guests would show up for breakfast. One room was occupied by a couple on a cross country trip for their honeymoon, and she hadn't seen much of them since they checked in two days ago. They seemed nice enough, but she got the feeling they wanted to be left alone.

She sliced the last of the strawberries, and took them and the freshly squeezed orange juice into the dining room. She was glad to have the distraction from thinking about Damian. She knew he would be en route by now, and she said a silent prayer for his safety. She wondered if he worried a little every time he got behind the wheel since his mother died in a car accident. She knew it would be later in the evening before he arrived, and she was hoping to get a pedicure before he got there.

After the morning rush, she told Vivian she was going into town for a few hours. She needed to get supplies and thought that was a good excuse to stop at the salon and get a pedicure while she was there. Vivian knew she was excited to see Damian. She only wondered how depressed she was going to be after he left in a few days. She had never seen Gina like this, and she knew she was falling in love with Damian, even if Gina wouldn't admit it to herself yet.

Damian had been on the road for nearly four hours. He had the radio tuned to the oldies that his mom had liked so much. It made him smile to sing along to the tunes he had heard since he was a boy. He had been thinking about Gina a lot and was a little nervous to see her again. He had packed some nicer clothes this time and was looking forward to spending some quality time with her. They had talked for hours on the phone and he felt like he knew her very well already. So far he hadn't found anything he didn't like about her, except her slightly different political views. But he was used to that. Being in the military and on the front lines often changed your view on things.

Damian was sad to lock up the house for the last time. The realtor had put the For Sale sign up yesterday, and it looked so odd in the front yard. He had taken the last of the boxes of things he wanted to keep to the storage unit and donated most of the rest. The house was empty now; he even went through and cleaned it. He asked the realtor to hire a lawn service and to check on things for him. He left his number in case he had any questions or got an offer on the house. He was glad he had this visit with Gina to look forward to or it would have been even harder to leave.

He had made peace with his mother for not telling him about his father. He could see how it would have been confusing for him to have the colonel in and out of his life depending on his duty stations. He also realized how difficult it would have been for his mother to see him if he had remained in their lives. His dad was a good man, and he had taken good care of them. He felt doubly blessed to have had his dad and now the colonel as his father. He didn't feel quite so alone in the world. He had talked to his father a couple of times, and made plans to meet in California in a few weeks. Dave was going to drive down to Camp Pendleton anyway for a meeting, so he would stay an extra couple of days and they could spend some time together. He had been stationed at Camp Pendleton about ten years ago, and he knew the area well. His daughter, Tessa, had changed plans for spring break, so Damian would not get to meet her for now. The colonel explained that he had wanted to tell her in person, so he was waiting for the right time.

Damian was hoping that if the other Marines discovered who his father was it wouldn't make a difference in his career or his friendships. He was his own man, and he didn't want to be judged by whom he happened to be related to. He had told his father as much, and he reassured him that he wasn't in the business of paving the way for anybody. "If you didn't earn it, then it isn't worth anything," Dave had said. Damian couldn't agree more.

Chapter Seventeen

As Damian pulled up in front of the Inn, the sun was just beginning to set. The sky was aglow with oranges and pinks that matched the beautiful rock formations that surrounded the area. Everything looked better to Damian this time. He wasn't sure if it was because the last time he was here he was so tired and stressed or if it was because he knew Gina was here. He was so glad he had taken the old guy's advice at the gas station and stopped here. No matter the outcome, he felt it had been a life changing decision in some way.

Oliver greeted Damian by rubbing up against his legs as he took his suitcase out of the car. "Hey, Oliver, you remember me, don't you?" Gina greeted Damian at the door with a hug. Her cheeks blushed red when he smiled at her.

"How was your drive?" Gina asked as she led the way inside.

"It was fine. The rock formations are beautiful around here, but even more so at sunset." Damian grinned from ear to ear.

"Are you hungry? I've got some leftover shepherd's pie in the refrigerator and some cherry cobbler." Gina returned the smile as she made her way into the kitchen.

"That sounds fabulous. How did you get to be such a great cook, by the way?" Damian sat down on a barstool as Gina took out a plate.

"I actually went to school to be a chef. I found it was a way for me to be creative and make people happy at the same time." Gina pulled out two wine glasses and offered him some wine with dinner. He opted for the red, and was surprised at how good the local wine tasted.

They talked while Damian ate, and then they went into the living room. There was a warm fire burning, giving it a cozy feeling. "I feel like I'm taking advantage of you, eating your food and staying here for a few days." Damian looked up as he took Gina's hand.

"Not at all, I'm the one who invited you to begin with, remember?" Gina loved the way their hands fit together. She knew she was blushing again.

Suddenly Damian grew serious. He looked at her and thought she was the most amazingly beautiful woman he had ever seen. He leaned over and brought her chin up with his fingers, caressing her cheek with his thumb. His mouth closed over hers, and it felt warm and soft. Gina reached up and ran her hand through his hair and it was as if her touch made him kiss her harder, with so much passion that it nearly took her breath away. Keeping his feelings in check, he pulled back from her but continued to caress her face. She opened her eyes to his dazzling smile and couldn't help but smile back at him.

"I've been thinking about that for weeks," Damian said matter-of-factly. Gina laughed at him.

"With all that has been on your mind, I'm honored that I crept in there at all." Gina squeezed his hand.

"Crept in there? You've practically taken over my thoughts." Damian wondered if that was something he should share right away, but he was honest to a fault.

Damian sat with his arms around her as they watched the fire burn down. It was so easy to be with her, and he was going to hate to leave in a few days. They made plans for going sightseeing the next day. Gina explained that Vivian was going to work extra hours so that they could spend some time together. He was touched that she had it all planned out. They were going on a picnic tomorrow and then to do some rock climbing the day after that. They finally said good night, and Gina showed him to his room. He kissed her again before watching her walk down the hall.

As he lay in bed looking up at the stars, he couldn't help but smile to himself. Kissing Gina had been even better than he imagined. He didn't want to rush things between them. He knew she was special, and he didn't want her to feel he only wanted one thing.

He knew he wanted her, but what he wanted most of all was her heart.

Gina had packed the perfect picnic. She and Damian hiked up to a vista that overlooked the desert, and the view was breathtaking. The sun was warm, but it wasn't hot and a few white fluffy clouds floated overhead. Gina had packed some brie and crackers, fresh fruit, and home-made tarts. She also had packed a bottle of wine and two glasses. Damian thought it was a far cry from the MRE's he usually ate out in the field, and the scenery was much more beautiful. She spread a blanket on the ground and proceeded to take the food out of the basket. He couldn't stop looking at her, and he reached out and touched her arm as she was setting things out for their lunch. "You are so beautiful." Damian smiled at Gina and made her stomach do a little flip.

"Thank you," Gina blushed. He took her in his arms and kissed her. The kiss was full of longing and passion, and Gina was sorry when it ended.

"Stop that, or we may never get to eat," she teased.

After lunch they hiked further back into the rocks. Damian found an area that he thought would be suitable for rock climbing. He was planning to teach Gina how to climb the next day. He decided he wouldn't do anything too complicated, like repelling off the rocks. *It wouldn't be much of a date if someone got hurt*, he thought. Damian was enjoying every minute of their time together. He knew he would be sorry to have to leave in a few days. At least he could drive to New Mexico for long weekends. It was hard for Gina to get away because of the Inn, but she said maybe she could fly out to see him for a weekend here or there. He was beginning to think that a few days now and then were never going to be enough for him.

The day flew by, and after dinner Damian took Gina by the hand and led her to the patio behind the Inn. The sun was setting, and there was a slight breeze. They sat on the glider with his arm around her and just enjoyed being together. Damian knew Gina would have to go in and prepare some things for breakfast soon, so he wanted to make the most of the time they had together. They talked a little about their families, and Gina told him a funny story about her brother. It was so easy being with her; he felt like he belonged there.

The next day Damian was up early and came down to help Gina with breakfast. He wasn't a great cook, but he could set the table and help out. After they finished, they headed out to the area they had seen yesterday to do some rock climbing. Damian was an experienced climber and Gina was eager to learn. She had always wanted to but had never had the time, she said.

Damian went over the basics of rock climbing. He stressed above all else, that you should never climb alone and should always let someone know where you are going. He knew she had told Vivian where they were going, so they had those bases covered. They began with an easy climb, and Damian was surprised how quickly Gina learned. She was keeping up with him and seemed to be a natural. The sun was warm and the sky a brilliant blue. They made it up to the first plateau area and stopped to decide which way to climb next.

Gina was really enjoying the climb. She was in excellent shape from doing yoga, and her body was toned. She asked Damian if they could attempt a more difficult climb. He thought she was learning fast enough, but didn't want her to get in over her head. It was difficult for him to resist her green eyes and warm smile, so he agreed to take her on a more difficult climb.

They headed up the next cliff face. It was definitely more difficult than the first climb. Damian told Gina to watch where he put his hands and feet and to follow his lead. He was going slowly, making sure she was close behind him.

All of a sudden, he heard pebbles falling. He looked back and could see that Gina had missed a foot hold and was trying to find a place to put her right foot. He talked to her very calmly, instructing her which way to feel for a foot hold. He told her not to look down; he was afraid she would freeze from the fear. He had served with men in the Corps who would almost get to the top of a cliff and suddenly be overtaken with fear once they looked down. Gina listened to him and struggled to find a place for her foot. Her hands ached from hanging on so tightly. She finally managed to get her foot in a good position, but her ankle was hurting badly. She had twisted it and banged it against the rocks.

Damian talked to her the rest of the way up, only a few more feet. He helped her over the edge and could see that she was hurt.

"Are you all right?" He asked as he looked at her. She was scared; he could see fear reflected in her eyes.

"I think so, except my ankle hurts. I twisted it trying to find that last foot hold." Gina tried to smile, but it was difficult through the pain. Damian knelt down and took a look at her ankle. It was swollen and bleeding from an abrasion caused by the rock. He told her to sit down, and he grabbed an ice pack from his backpack and placed it on her ankle. Gina winced, but in a few minutes the cold was numbing the pain.

Damian proceeded to take an ace bandage and tape out of his backpack, and wrapped it around Gina's ankle, encompassing the ice pack. He was looking over the rock they had just climbed and he could see a walking path. It was a longer way down, but they had no choice. Gina couldn't continue to climb with her ankle injured.

Damian was so concerned about Gina. He apologized to her for getting her injured. She assured him it wasn't his fault, but he still felt guilty. He went against his better judgment and took her on a climb she wasn't ready for, something that went against all of his training. She was impressed that he had a full-blown first aid kit with him and that he knew exactly what to do.

He wasn't intimidated by a little blood like some guys she knew.

Damian picked Gina up and headed toward the trail. She protested loudly, saying that she was able to walk, but he would not hear of it. She felt a little silly, but at the same time she was touched that he cared about her so much. She finally stopped protesting because she could tell he wasn't going to change his mind. Besides, she knew it would make it harder for him to carry her if she wasn't cooperating.

They made it back to his car and Damian checked her ankle again. He had tried his best to keep it elevated, but it was a difficult task on the walk down. Her ankle was still swollen, but it had stopped bleeding. "Tell me which way to go to get you to a hospital so we can have your ankle checked." Damian lifted her as he helped her into the car.

"I don't want to go to a hospital. I'm sure if you would take me by the clinic, they would see me. One of the doctors is my friend." Gina tried to find a position for her leg to lessen the pain, but was not successful.

"Okay, then, tell me which way to go to get you to the clinic." Damian got in and started the car.

Once they were back at the Inn, Damian made Gina put her foot up. Dr. Taylor had said nothing was broken but a bad sprain just the same. Damian felt horrible. Not only did she get hurt while she was with him, now it was going to be difficult for her to do her job on crutches. Gina had already talked to Vivian, and she was going to work extra to help out. She had also called her mother, and she said she would be there in a couple of days to help run the Inn until she could get back on her feet—literally. Dr. Taylor had given Gina some pain medication, but she refused to take anything stronger than ibuprofen. Damian admired her for that, but still felt guilty that she was injured in the first place.

Now that Gina was not able to move around much, they decided to try and make the most of the two days they had left to spend together. Damian helped Vivian with the cooking with Gina's supervision. He also went into town for supplies and fed Oliver. Damian wouldn't let her do much of anything, and he was always so gentle with her. Gina thought that someday he would make a good father. He was patient and kind and had a good heart. She knew she was starting to fall in love with him, and, even though her head told her no, her heart refused to listen.

They spent the evenings on the patio sipping wine and talking. They never seemed to run out of things to say. She tried to tell him it was all her fault she sprained her ankle, because she wanted to do a more difficult climb. He refused to let her take the blame, which she thought was very noble of him. The evenings were warm, but it wasn't too hot yet. They stayed out on the patio after dark to look through Gina's telescope at the stars. It was a passion of hers that he loved and found he looked forward to trying to find the constellations each night.

On their last evening together, they were both quiet. Neither of them knew where this relationship was going, but they both felt certain that they didn't want it to end. Damian held Gina in his arms and stroked her hair. "I really don't want to leave tomorrow." Damian stroked her cheek with his thumb as he brushed her hair back from her face.

"I don't want you to go, but I guess that is the way it is when Uncle Sam needs you." Gina sounded a little more sarcastic than she meant to. She was beginning to realize that a life with Damian would be a series of good-byes, and she wasn't sure she could deal with that. *It's going to be hard enough to say good-bye tomorrow, what if he were leaving to go fight a war overseas somewhere? What if there was a real possibility he would not return?* she wondered.

Damian could sense that Gina was pulling away from him. He had been honest with her about what life in the Marine Corps meant. It was full of sacrifices for all involved. He was also honest enough to let her know it was what he had chosen as a career, and he didn't plan on giving it up. He wanted her to know that a woman would have to love him enough to let him live the life he had chosen, however difficult it may be. He tried to make her see that if he gave up the Marine Corps then it would be giving up his dream. She understood, but wasn't sure if she could make that kind of sacrifice. She had stayed awake thinking about it, and decided as much as it would break her heart now, it would be better than more heartache down the road. A clean break would be easiest she decided, but somehow her heart didn't agree. She was trying to find a way to say as much to Damian, but he had been so wonderful; she just couldn't find the words.

"You know, Gina, I've never felt this way about anyone. I know you don't want to hear this, but I think I'm falling in love with you. I can tell that you think it would be easier if we just parted ways now. You think it would be too hard to be with a Marine, and I've been brutally honest with you about that." Gina swallowed hard. She was amazed that he had been able to sense what she couldn't bring herself to say. "But taking the easy way isn't always the best way. I can promise you that if you will give me a chance that I will do everything in my power to make sure you don't regret that decision. I think what we have is rare, and I don't want to throw it away because you think it would be easier." Damian took her hands in his and looked into her eyes. There were tears waiting to be shed, and Gina couldn't speak.

He lifted her face to his and kissed her gently, and then held her in his arms. When Gina found her voice, she turned to Damian.

"You are a mind reader, aren't you? I was trying to find a way to tell you that this would be easier if we ended it now. This has been unlike anything I've ever felt, and I feel sick when I think about you leaving. But the thought of having to feel this way every time you go away is awful too. I'm really confused right now. My head says one thing but my heart another." Gina rested her head on his shoulder.

"If you can honestly tell me that you don't love me, then I will walk out of your life tomorrow and will never bother you again." Damian's words stung her heart. "But if you feel about me as I do about you then I think that the easy way isn't the right way, at least not for us. Take a chance on me, on us. Let's see where things go."

Damian's lips were on her mouth with an eagerness and hardness she hadn't expected. She was breathless when he finally released her. Her head kept telling her to walk away, but somewhere deep in her heart she knew she had to give it a chance. She had never felt this way about anyone, and she just couldn't turn her back on Damian.

"Okay," Gina said timidly.

"What did you say?" Damian asked.

"I said, okay. As in, okay, let's see where this goes." Gina smiled as she tried to reposition her foot.

"You have made me the happiest man on earth." Damian hugged her tightly. "You won't regret it." He scooped her up and carried her inside the Inn.

Chapter Eighteen

Frank hurried into his office to answer the phone. He had just walked in the door and was in the process of taking off his jacket. "Frank Webster," he growled as he put down his briefcase. He couldn't imagine who was calling him so early in the day.

"Frank, this is Kate West. We met at the Blue Moon Inn, and you gave me your business card. Do you remember me?" Kate felt awkward calling Frank, but she wanted to cover all of her bases before buying the flower shop.

"Kate, yes, how are you?" Frank sat down and took out a pen. He figured this must be a business call and not for pleasure. "I'm fine, actually better than fine. I'm pregnant." Kate laughed as she said it. She couldn't believe she was telling this to someone she barely knew, but somehow it just seemed right. Frank had been so kind to her when she was at the Blue Moon Inn; she wanted to share the good news.

"Congratulations. I guess now we know why you weren't feeling like eating much when you were at the Inn." Frank chuckled.

"Yes, now we know. Listen, Frank, I have the opportunity to buy a business. A flower shop, to be more exact. I've got some financial papers that I would like you to take a look at. I'd be glad to pay you for your time." Kate hoped he would agree to review them for her, as she didn't want to take them to anyone at the bank because then they would know she was considering leaving her job.

"I'd be glad to take a look at them. Why don't you fax them over to me, and I will try and look at them sometime today and get back with you in the morning." Frank was smiling and taking notes. He loved his job as an accountant, even if it wasn't glamorous.

"Thank you so much, Frank. I truly appreciate it," Kate sighed with relief.

"Kate, by the way, there is no fee. I hope it all works out for you, I think you would be a great business owner." Frank gave Kate his fax number and his home number in case she needed to reach him after hours. Kate couldn't believe her good fortune to have met such a nice person that was willing to help her.

Frank was glad to hear from Kate, even if it was to ask for a favor. He had genuinely liked her and had sensed a sadness about her. She sounded so happy about her pregnancy. A slight pang pierced his heart as he thought about the children he would never have. He had wanted at least two, but Carol wouldn't hear of it. *Now, it's too late*, he thought. He made himself a few more notes to put with the fax that was coming in from Kate. He planned to take a look at it when he got a chance later in the day. Kate seemed like a sensible woman that would not jump into something lightly. He hoped this business venture would be a wise decision for her, but he was going to be honest with her. If he felt it was too much of a risk, he would tell her that.

Frank had seen Maggie a couple of times in the past two weeks. Their relationship was progressing, but he still sensed that she was holding back. He knew that this was all new to her to be dating again. He also knew she felt a loyalty to Neal even though he was gone. He had to admire her for that, even if it meant that he would have to be patient. They were planning to meet at his place this weekend and go see an art exhibit and have dinner. He told Maggie that she was welcome to stay overnight, and even promised to be a perfect gentleman if she decided to stay. She said she would think about it, but he could hear the hesitancy in her voice.

Frank tried to push thoughts of Maggie out of his mind. He knew he was falling in love with her, but he was not sure if she felt the same about him. He didn't know if he was willing to put his heart out there for a woman who just wasn't capable of returning his love. He thought that in time, she would change her mind and not be so guarded. He only hoped he could wait that long.

Kate was getting more excited as she thought about the prospect of owning her own flower shop. She was trying not to get her hopes up until she heard from Frank. She had run the numbers herself, but she wanted someone else to give her an opinion. She was not one to do things lightly. She had to be certain she was making the right decision.

Things between her and Matt had improved slightly. He was surprised when she told him that she had spoken with the owner of the flower shop and had gotten the financial information to review. She could tell that he thought this was something she should pursue, and she was grateful to him for his support. She just didn't want to rush into something she would regret later. But she was learning life didn't come with any guarantees, and it was impossible to plan out every detail as much as she preferred it.

She had been to see Dr. Yang again and this time she was able to hear the baby's heartbeat. Matt had gone with her, and both of them were excited and relieved that the pregnancy was progressing well. Kate had cried when she heard the baby's heartbeat; she just couldn't help herself. The next visit to see Dr. Yang was to have an ultrasound, and she told them they needed to decide if they wanted to know the sex of the baby.

LISA SAMSON

Of course she wanted to know so they could plan the nursery and pick out names, but Matt was not so sure. He felt that not finding out until the baby was born was one of those great moments in life. He thought that knowing ahead of time was like cheating, and he didn't want to know until the time came.

Kate knew that if she knew and Matt didn't that she would let it slip somehow and ruin it for him. In one way Kate thought that if she didn't know the sex of the baby, she wouldn't be as attached to it in case something happened. But with every passing day, she knew she was only kidding herself. She talked to the baby often and could feel the slightest stirring movements inside her. It felt like a butterfly floating deep within her, and the sensation always made her smile. The nausea had improved since she had started on the medication Dr. Yang had prescribed, and she was able to eat normally again. Matt was very glad about that, he was beginning to lose weight because he couldn't eat anything with an aroma for fear of making her sick.

Matt had taken over cooking duty now that she was feeling better, and was even doing more around the house. He was kind to her, but seemed distant when she talked about the baby. He went out often in the evenings now, saying he was meeting friends or going back to the office to catch up on work. She had told her colleagues and most of their family about the baby now. Everyone was extremely happy for them, and friends were already making plans for baby showers. She told Matt that if they knew the sex of the baby it would make it easier for people to buy gifts. He said they could buy green or yellow things. He wasn't going to change his mind. She loved Matt, but he was very stubborn at times.

She didn't want to start talking about names for the baby just yet. It was all kind of surreal to her still. She had considered naming it Gina if it was a girl, because she had been so wonderful to her when she was at the Blue Moon Inn. They had become friends, and they talked on the phone and e-mailed each other. She knew that she was spending a few days with Damian, so she was waiting to call her until after he left. She had a feeling she was going to be a little down, and she hoped she could help cheer her a little.

Gina was the kind of person you could bare your soul to and not worry that she was going to judge you or tell others. She had an easiness about her that she didn't find with many of her other friends. She had told Matt about how much she had helped her while she was in New Mexico, and he said he would like to meet her some day. She was hoping to take a trip to the Blue Moon Inn before the baby was born. But if she was going to buy the flower shop that might be a little more difficult.

Kate had not said anything to anyone at work about the flower shop. She had applied for a small business loan through a friend of hers that worked at another bank. She had decided that if she did pur-chase the flower shop she would keep the two women who worked part-time as part of her staff. One lady was a lovely older woman with a keen sense of style. Her name was Helen. She wasn't the fastest, but she was meticulous, and Kate instantly liked her. She had been working at the flower shop for five years, and the owner said she had been a model employee. The other lady worked more during their busier seasons, helping with weddings mostly. She also came in for a few hours every day and made deliveries around town. She seemed quiet and reserved, and her name was Jody. She had been working there about two years and appeared to be in her late thirties. She didn't smile much, but the owner said she had been reliable.

She sincerely hoped that neither of them would mind if she brought the baby into the shop for a few hours a day. She really liked the idea of being able to do that and thought it would make nursing much easier. She had talked to a few friends about finding a sitter, once the baby arrived. She didn't like the idea of leaving her baby at a large daycare; she was hoping to find someone who would watch only her child. Her friends warned her that child care was expensive, and she needed to budget accordingly. Kate was hoping maybe she could find a grandmotherly type, who would adore her baby. She had put it on her calendar to start contacting some of the referrals an agency had given her. She didn't want to put it off, but felt it was too soon to be hiring someone. Matt was off on Wednesday afternoons, so he could watch the baby then. She could take the baby to work with her on Wednesday mornings, she reasoned, and that way they would only need a sitter four days a week.

She was starting to feel less tired, and more like her old self. She even stayed up to watch the news the last two nights, and Matt had joked how impressed he was. She was taking daily walks and naps whenever she could. The prenatal vitamins were staying down, and she had gained three pounds at her last visit with Dr. Yang. She knew she would need to purchase some maternity clothes soon. Her mother had offered to take her shopping on Saturday, and she was looking forward to it. When she felt stressed, she would close her eyes and envision the patio at the Blue Moon Inn. She tried to imagine the sounds of the fountain and the birds singing. Somehow this seemed to soothe her, and she found she longed to go back to the Blue Moon again. It was one of the most peaceful places on earth.

Chapter Nineteen

Damian had crossed the state line into California, and he was still thinking about Gina. Although she had agreed to give their relationship a chance, he knew she did so hesitantly. It was the first time since he had joined the Marine Corps that he questioned his decision to make it his career. He knew it would be much easier on their relationship if he had a regular job. But somehow he just couldn't imagine being happy with himself, even if Gina was. He knew himself well enough to know that he wasn't going to give up the Corps. He hoped Gina would care about him enough to give them a chance, but if she didn't he would deal with it. At least that is what he told himself.

Damian had enjoyed every minute at the Blue Moon Inn. He felt terrible that Gina had sprained her ankle, and still felt responsible. He thought about their time together and it made him smile. He loved sitting out on the patio in the evenings, just waiting for the stars to appear. The desert had a different feel and rhythm; it made him slow down and enjoy life somehow. He was going to try and see Gina in a few weeks, but until then the phone would have to be enough. Hearing her voice was no substitute for holding her and touching her, but right now he didn't have a choice.

He tried to focus on his new duty station. He had heard the San Diego area was beautiful and was looking forward to being stationed there. It would be nice to be stateside instead of overseas. He had talked with the colonel. He still couldn't bring himself to call him Dave, or Dad, but he was working on it. The colonel had already accepted his next command post in Twentynine Palms and was settling in. They had planned to meet the next weekend in San Diego and spend the day together looking around the area. Damian hoped that Gina would get to meet his father soon. He had talked to him at length about Gina, and he had given him some good advice. He told him to take it slow, and not let his good judgment go out the window. He was doing his best to follow that advice, but it was difficult.

Damian thought about his mom and decided that she would have liked Gina. He was sorry that they would never get to meet each other, and it made his sense of loss keener as he thought about it. He hoped he had done the right thing, putting the house up for sale. He knew that he would not be able to live there any time in the near future, and he didn't want to have to worry about renting it to someone. In his mind, selling it was the most logical thing to do. He made a mental note to call the realtor next week to see if anyone had even looked at the house. He had priced it based on the realtor's recommendations, as he had no idea what the house was worth.

Again Damian's thoughts turned to Gina. He began to wonder how their relationship could grow, with him in California and her in New Mexico. Because she ran the Inn, it was difficult for her to get away at all. He would be free most weekends, but it was too far to drive just for a weekend, and flying back and forth would get expensive. Maybe Gina was right, and they should just go their separate ways. But the thought of that made him feel sick, and he knew that what they shared was too special to let slip away. He would have to find a way to give their relationship a chance.

In New Mexico, Gina was hopping around the kitchen without her crutches. She decided they slowed her down too much when she was trying to cook. Her mother had come to help and she was grateful. Vivian was working extra too, so between the three of them things were running smoothly. Gina was going back to the doctor tomorrow to check on her ankle. She was hoping she wouldn't have to use the crutches anymore.

Gina cried when Damian left, and had been sad ever since. Kate had called her the day he left and tried to lift her spirits. She appreciated the distraction, but still missed Damian terribly. She had not expected to feel this way, and she wondered how long it would take for this feeling to go away. She tried to go on with business as usual, but she felt like a part of her was missing. She had thought about it so much that she was losing sleep. She just didn't see how they were going to be able to spend much time together. For the first time since she came to run the Inn, she was wondering if this was what she wanted to continue to do. She loved running the Inn, she only wished it was located closer to Damian. They had talked on the phone, but she didn't bring up her concerns. He knew her thoughts, but she had agreed to give them a chance. The more she thought about it, the more difficult it became for her to envision her life without him.

Gina had talked to her mom and Kate about it, and both of them said to give it some time and see what happens. Gina's mom said she had talked to her sister, who owned the Inn. They had been traveling around the country in their RV and were headed back to New Mexico, she said. Of course they would stop and see whatever they wanted along the way, so it might take some time before they were back. They were in Florida when she had called.

Gina took a cup of tea and hopped out the door and onto the back patio. She loved to sit out there and enjoy the birds. It was also a favorite place to hang out with Damian, and she felt closer to him when she was out there. She propped her leg up on a small table, enjoying the relief from the throbbing in her ankle. It was healing, but it was still swollen and blue. Dr. Taylor had told her that a bad sprain was sometimes worse than a break and not to expect it to heal completely for a few weeks.

She closed her eyes and could almost feel Damian's arms around her. She could hear his voice and smell his cologne if she concentrated hard enough. It was no substitute for having him there, but it was all she had for now. *This is what it will be like every time he deploys*, she thought. But at least she would have the hope of him returning to her. Could she live with the uncertainty that he might not return? Could she be the kind of wife that would support her husband throughout his military career? What if they had children, how would they adjust to moving so frequently, and having their father gone so much? These were tough questions that she just couldn't answer. She knew many families lived this life every day. She just wasn't sure she could be one of them.

Just then, the back door swung open, interrupting her thoughts. Vivian had come to tell her she was going to get supplies and asked her if she needed anything. "No, thanks." Gina forced a smile as she said it. *What I need you can't get in town,* she thought.

Chapter Twenty

Maggie had enjoyed Elizabeth's visit over spring break. She and her boyfriend had worked things out, so she was in better spirits. They had gone shopping, out to eat, and watched movies, and Maggie had loved every minute of it. It was always hard when she went back to college; Maggie had to adjust to the loneliness all over again.

Maggie had told Elizabeth about Frank and was surprised by her reaction. She had expected her to be upset about her dating, but instead she was very supportive. She thought it was about time that she got on with her life. She reminded her that she was not dead, and that her dad would have wanted her to be happy. Maggie had thought about introducing Frank to Elizabeth, but she just wasn't quite ready. She didn't want to miss any opportunity to spend time with Elizabeth so she had asked Frank to set their plans aside while she was home from college.

After Elizabeth went back to school, she was determined to start going through Neal's things. She was standing in the living room surrounded by boxes but felt like she didn't know where to begin. Her instinct was to get in the car and drive far away, but she knew it was time to deal with his things. The first step is the hardest, she told herself.

She decided to start with something small. She went over to the table in the living room that was by the chair where he always sat. She pulled out the drawer and began going through the papers and magazines that he had stored there. After that, she decided to go through his file cabinet in the office. It took her most of the morning, and by lunch time she was feeling proud of herself. She had only cried once, which was better than she thought she would do. It felt good to finally go through his things. She thought maybe there were some items that Elizabeth might want, and she was putting those things aside for her.

After grabbing a sandwich in the kitchen, Maggie decided to continue. The only room she had left was their bedroom. Neal had his own closet and was never very organized. She knew it was going to take some time to go through everything.

She was making good progress. She had gone through Neal's clothes, and now was sorting through the boxes. There were several boxes filled with papers and receipts. She started to put all of them in the trash, when a letter fell out. She looked at the handwriting and didn't recognize it. She pulled out the letter and began reading. She fell to her knees in shock. Her hands began to tremble as she continued to read.

My darling Neal,

It pained me so to see you go this morning. Last night was incredible, and I am smiling now just thinking about it. I know you feel a loyalty to your wife and baby, but I just don't think she loves you like I do. If you were happy there, you wouldn't have been with me. What we have shared has been special and wonderful, and you know I love you. I also hope that you love me. You make me feel things I have never felt before. You are, and always will be, the man for me. If you ever change your mind, and I'm hoping you will, I will be waiting for you with open arms.

Always,
Bella

Maggie sat on the floor completely stunned. She wondered how she could not have known. She thought back to the time right before Elizabeth was born. Things were very tight financially, and she was working to get established as a writer. She was trying to finish college at night. Neal was working, but they were barely making ends meet, and he was very frustrated because the pregnancy had not been planned. He wanted to travel and see the world before they had children, and was not quite ready to settle into parent-hood. They had been married less than a year and were arguing constantly. She remembered that he was gone more than usual, but he always told her he was working extra hours. Now she finally knew the truth.

After Elizabeth was born, things eventually settled into a routine. Maggie's writing career was taking off, which eased their financial situation considerably. Neal adored Elizabeth and started coming home earlier to spend more time with her. They had also gone to a few counseling sessions but had to stop because their insurance wouldn't cover any more. She couldn't believe that she had not suspected anything. She thought she knew Neal as well as she knew herself, but apparently she had been wrong.

Maggie read the letter again. *Who was Bella?* She couldn't think of any friends they had that went by Bella or Isabel. Maybe it was someone he worked with, but she couldn't remember him talking about anyone with that name. She couldn't imagine how Neal could have lived with himself all those years without telling her. She wondered now if their whole relationship had been a lie.

Suddenly, Maggie was furious. She wanted answers to questions that only a dead man could know. *How could he do this to me!* she raged in her mind. She began to throw boxes and papers everywhere and scream at Neal as if he were standing in the room. She collapsed in a heap and sobbed for what seemed like hours.

As the sun was setting and darkness began to overtake the room, Maggie got up off the floor. She didn't know what to do next, so she simply left the mess and walked out of the bedroom, closing the door behind her. She grabbed her car keys and headed out the door. She couldn't bear to be in the house she had lived in with Neal for another minute. She wasn't sure she ever wanted to return.

Maggie felt the wind on her face as she drove the convertible a little faster than she should. It felt good to be out on the open road with her hair wild and free. She didn't know where she was headed, but she knew she couldn't stay in that house. She floored the accelerator and rounded the next corner, tears stinging her eyes. She had been betrayed by the man she trusted above all others; how would she ever trust again? She thought about calling Frank, but she didn't feel like talking to anyone except Neal, but that was impossible now.

Maggie drove for a couple of hours until she needed to stop and get gas. She pulled into a station, not even realizing the route she had driven or where she was. As she was putting gas in her car, she looked up, and there was a sign for the Blue Moon Inn. Maggie took it as an omen. She would spend the night there if Gina had a room for her, and maybe in the morning she could think more clearly. She hopped back into her car and took the next exit. Up ahead she could see the Inn. It was all lit up inside; it looked welcoming.

She pulled up to the Inn and got out. She kept a small suitcase in the back with a change of clothes and a makeup bag in it, just in case she got stranded some-where. She was grateful for that now. She grabbed the suitcase and headed inside. Oliver greeted her at the door as if he remembered her. He rubbed his head on her leg and began to purr. "At least you like me," Mag-gie muttered as she stepped into the foyer.

Gina came around the corner on her crutches. "Maggie! How are you?" Gina said with a warm smile. She pretended not to notice her tear stained face and disheveled hair.

"Gina, what happened to your leg?" Maggie asked trying to avoid her question.

"I sprained my ankle trying to rock climb. It was not one of my best moments. But I'm going back to the doctor tomorrow and hoping I can get rid of these things." Gina gestured to her crutches.

"I know how you feel. I broke my leg once trying to snow ski and was on crutches for six weeks. They are no fun, and they made my arms hurt." Maggie tried to smile. It suddenly occurred to her how ridiculous she must look. Her hair was a mess, her mascara was surely smeared and her eyes were red and puffy from cry-ing. Gina had noticed but didn't say anything. Mag-gie loved that about her. She figured if Maggie wanted to talk about it, she would. She wondered if she and Frank had an argument.

"I was hoping I could stay here tonight, if you have a room available." Maggie looked hopefully at Gina.

"Of course, let me get you a key." Gina hopped over to the desk and took out the key to Maggie's room.

"Stay as long as you need to, Maggie." Gina looked her in the eye when she said it, as if to say she understood.

"Thank you. I'm sorry I didn't call ahead for a reservation, but it was kind of a spur of the moment thing," Maggie said apologetically.

"That's fine; don't worry about it. I've got some leftover meatloaf if you're hungry." Suddenly, Maggie realized she hadn't eaten a thing since lunch. But somehow the thought of food was not appealing.

"No, but thank you anyway." Maggie picked up her bag and headed upstairs.

Once inside the room, Maggie sat her bag down and plopped on the bed. The room was decorated in burgundies and gold tones and there was a cozy quilt draped over the chair near the bed. She gazed up through the skylight at the million stars that seemed to be in her view. She didn't know what to do next but hoped that somehow she could make peace with the information she had discovered. Maybe she needed to call her therapist when she got back home. *Home. That had a strange sound to it now.* She suddenly felt like her house wasn't her home anymore. She had shared that home with Neal and raised their daughter there, but now it felt like it was all a charade somehow. She had thought that Neal was the most wonderful man she had ever known but now her dream was shattered. Hadn't they been one of those rare couples that were happily married? Sure, they had their rough patches, but what couple didn't? She felt like she couldn't trust her judgment about men and wondered if Frank had cheated on his wife too.

Maggie decided to take a hot shower. As the water poured over her body, she thought about Frank. She really liked him and thought perhaps they could have a future together. Now, she thought it would be easier to be alone than to have to put her heart on the line. She was angry, not just at Neal but at herself. Maybe somewhere in the back of her mind she had known the truth, but without any evidence she didn't have to face it. Now, there was no turning back. She knew for certain Neal had been unfaithful, and it was more than a one night stand. *How am I ever going to make peace with that?*

Maggie climbed into bed but knew sleep would not come easily. She gazed up at the brilliant stars. Even though she knew there would be no answers, she began to talk to Neal. She asked him why he had cheated on her, and how he could have kept it a secret all these years. She asked him if he had ended it, or if he had been unfaithful the entire time they were married. She raged at him and punched her pillow. Finally, out of exhaustion, she fell into a fitful sleep.

When morning came the bright sunlight streamed through the window. She could hear the birds chirping and smell blueberry muffins. It reminded her of waking up on Saturday mornings as a child. She felt safe here, and wondered how she would ever go back home. She had a knot in her stomach, but it was growling so she went downstairs to try and eat something. She didn't want Gina to worry about her.

She dressed in the only clothes she had brought with her, washed her face and brushed her teeth. She smoothed down her unruly tresses and went downstairs. "Good morning." An older lady greeted her as she took a seat in the dining room.

Maggie returned the greeting, but she wondered where Gina was. The woman must have seen the confused look on her face.

"I'm Gina's mom. I'm here to help out until Gina gets back on both feet." She smiled and extended her hand.

"I'm Maggie. Breakfast smells wonderful," She helped herself to a cup of steaming hot coffee. Gina's mom went back into the kitchen, and soon reappeared with a basket of blueberry muffins, crisp bacon, fresh melon, and orange juice. She could see that a few other guests had already eaten breakfast, so she guessed she would be dining alone. It didn't matter that much to her anymore, she had become accustomed to it.

Maggie was suddenly very hungry. She ate two muffins, a slice of bacon and some fruit. She finished with a large glass of orange juice. Now that her stomach was satisfied, she had to decide what to do next. She wasn't ready to go home and face the boxes of Neal's things again. She felt like she wanted to start over. To sell the house, get rid of everything, and start fresh. She wondered how Elizabeth would feel about that. Because she was a freelance writer she could work from anywhere, and the thought of moving to a new place suddenly excited her.

Just then Gina came through the door. She wasn't using crutches and had only a small air cast on her ankle. She was limping only slightly.

"You must have gotten good news at the doctor today," Maggie said after she remembered Gina mentioning it the night before.

"Great news! I can officially walk without the crutches. She said my ankle was healing nicely, and that I could be on my feet a little more now." Gina hobbled over to a chair across from Maggie and sat down. "How are you?" She looked her right in the eye.

"Hanging in there, I guess," Maggie said, averting her gaze.

Suddenly tears spilled over on Maggie's cheeks. She choked on a sob as Gina handed her a tissue.

"Would you like to go out on the patio with me?" Gina gently guided Maggie in that direction. Maggie could only nod as she tried to control her crying. Once outside they took a seat on the glider. Maggie had gained control of herself by then, and Gina just sat next to her in case she wanted to talk.

"You must think I'm ridiculous, crying like a baby."

"Not ridiculous, just someone who is hurting." She waited for Maggie to tell her more.

"Where do I begin?" Maggie said as she dabbed her eyes with a tissue.

"How about the beginning."

Maggie told Gina about Neal. How they met, married, and built a life together. She smiled as she talked about him and Elizabeth. Then she explained how she finally got the courage to go through his things and came upon the letter. How she felt like she had been betrayed and wanted answers, but there was nobody to answer her questions. How she was angry and wanted to run away, and now she didn't even want to go back home and had thought of moving.

"What if he had been unfaithful right in that very house, in our bedroom?" Maggie cried as she had not thought of that before. Gina listened and offered tissues as Maggie poured out her heart. She could not imagine the heartbreak she was feeling.

Finally when Maggie was finished, Gina put a hand on hers. "Maggie, from everything you have told me, it seems to me that Neal was a good man. He made a mistake, a huge one, but he must have ended the affair. I read that one of the times in a man's life when he is most vulnerable to cheating is when he is about to become a father. The responsibility overwhelms him. I'm not making excuses for him, but I know he wasn't the first man to cheat, and he won't be the last. He must have carried this secret and the guilt with him the rest of his life. Maybe the reason he never told you about it was because he didn't want to hurt you, and he didn't want to lose you. If he had wanted the other woman he would not have stayed with you."

"I hadn't thought of it that way." Maggie looked stunned.

"Maggie, what Neal did was horrible. But you have to try and forgive him, in order to move on. Holding onto this bitterness will only hurt you. It won't affect him." Gina was trying to be reasonable about the situation.

"I know you are right, but it is just difficult. This has been such a shock," Maggie said.

"Give yourself some time to heal, Maggie. By the way, whatever happened to Frank? I thought you two hit it off when you were here." Gina smiled, and her face brightened.

"We did hit it off. Actually, we have been dating. I even felt guilty about that, like I was cheating on Neal. Can you believe it? I bet I won't feel that way anymore." Maggie got up from the glider and began to pace. "I was so angry that I really considered giving up on men all together, including Frank. I thought that none of them could be trusted." She stopped pacing and then began to laugh. She realized how absurd that sounded once she said it. Gina laughed with her.

Gina and Maggie went inside and got some lemonade. Maggie asked Gina if she could stay another night at the Inn. Gina told her to stay as long as she liked. Maggie decided to go into town and do some shopping. If she was going to stay another night, she needed some more clothes. Besides, she thought the distraction would do her good.

As she was driving into town, she suddenly remembered she was supposed to call Frank last night to talk about their weekend plans. She quickly checked her cell and could see there were several calls from him and two voice mails. She didn't know if she would be very good company, but she at least owed it to him to return his call. She pulled into a parking space in front of a boutique. She hoped she could find something that was her style.

Before going into shop, she quickly phoned Frank. She knew he would be at work and wouldn't answer his cell phone. She knew it was cowardly, but it was the best she could do. She left a brief message saying how sorry she was, but that something had come up and she had forgotten to call. She also said that their weekend plans were still on if he was available. She didn't say she would call him later, as she didn't really feel like talking to him just yet.

Maggie walked into the boutique and was greeted by smells of jasmine and lavender. The shop was lovely, with a mixture of modern and southwest clothing. There was also a small area with jewelry made by local artists. Maggie found a bracelet that she loved. It was made of tiny stones of different colors, with small pieces of turquoise intermingled. She also found a necklace she was sure Elizabeth would like and decided to buy it for her birthday. She tried on a few outfits and finally settled on a pair of jeans and white blouse. The blouse had tiny turquoise colored beads accenting the collar, and it brought out the blue in her eyes.

By the time she finished shopping, she was feeling a little better. She walked down the street and sat on the bench where she and Frank had sat on their first date.

She thought about him and wondered if he would be unfaithful to her if they ever got married. She decided that there was no way to know who might cheat and that she couldn't judge Frank based on Neal's sins. She felt bad for not calling him the night before and genuinely hoped she didn't worry him. The thought of getting married again was something Maggie had rarely thought about, that is until now. For some reason she was extremely tired of being alone. She felt in a sense like a weight had been lifted somehow. Maybe Neal was giving her a final gift. It was the gift of freedom to move on with her life and not feel guilty about finding love again.

Maggie's spirit was lighter as she drove back to the Inn. It felt like she was going back to an old friend. She was so grateful for Gina. She had given her some insight into the situation and helped her put things in perspective. Maggie had told her if she ever tired of running the Inn she certainly would make a great therapist.

Chapter Twenty-One

Frank had finished looking over the financial papers Kate had faxed to him. From what he could tell, the flower shop was a thriving and profitable business. Kate had said that the owner suffered from arthritis, and it was just getting too painful for her to continue working. Frank had called Kate the previous evening and shared his findings with her. He joked that if she didn't buy the flower shop, he was going to buy it himself. He could hear the relief in her voice. He had a feeling that Kate was very organized and that she would find a way to make it work.

He was disturbed that Maggie had not answered her phone. He had left her a message and tried reaching her several times. He finally gave up and went to bed. He hoped she was all right. He worried more about her safety than she did, but he felt protective toward her all the same.

There was a new woman working in his office named Elaine. She seemed nice, and she had started stopping by Frank's office a few times a day, just to say hello, or tell him something funny that had happened. Frank didn't mind the distraction, and Elaine was certainly attractive. He had heard from one of the assistants that she had recently separated from her husband.

He still thought that Maggie was beautiful, but he had to admit that Elaine got his attention. Besides he hadn't seen Maggie in almost two weeks. She had been busy with Elizabeth on spring break. He still detected a wall that Maggie had erected around her heart, and he was seriously wondering if he would ever be able to break through it. He could easily fall head over heels for her, but he was trying not to get his heart broken again. Maggie was fun and interesting, but she was somewhat aloof. He enjoyed her company, but he wanted more from her. He wanted her heart, but he knew that it still belonged to Neal. He feared that it would always would.

Frank decided to try and concentrate on some work that needed to be completed before he went home. He didn't like to leave things until the next day if possible. It often meant he had to work late, but at least he didn't worry about work once he went home. He decided that he would wait and see if Maggie called him to confirm their plans for the weekend. He felt like he had been the one pursuing her, and he decided that if she wanted him, she could come to him.

Maggie slept more peacefully the second night at the Inn. She and Gina had a nice conversation over a cup of tea after dinner. She was so insightful, and Maggie was glad that she had ended up at the Blue Moon Inn again. She wondered if it was fate that had brought her there. She had thought more about Frank and decided he was a nice, kind, and decent man, and she genuinely liked him. She thought if she could let her guard down, she might even discover a definite physical attraction as well. She was planning on calling him once she returned home. It would give her something to look forward to other than dealing with Neal's things.

Gina's mom decided to return to California at the end of the week. Gina was getting around well without the crutches, and she and Vivian seemed to have things under control. Gina had told her mom about Damian and her concerns about falling in love with a military man. Her mother surprised her with her answer.

Gina's mother told her about a man she was deeply in love with before she met her father. He had been in the Navy, and his name was Charles. They had met at a local dance, and she was crazy about him. They wanted to get married, but her parents insisted it would never work. They thought that he would be unfaithful to her because he would be out at sea for months at a time. They also worried that he would get killed in the line of duty and leave her a widow with children to raise.

LISA SAMSON

Charles had begged her to elope with him. In the end she couldn't go against her parents' wishes, and she broke off her relationship with Charles.

She assured Gina that she loved her father very much and had a wonderful life with him. But, she added, she did wonder from time to time what her life would have been like with Charles. Gina's mom thought it would be exciting to live in different places and perhaps get to see the world. She knew it would have been difficult to be apart but thought that she would have been capable of handling things while he was away. She also reminded Gina that with all of the modern technology they could keep in touch much easier than in her day. They could email, or use a web cam; not wait for letters to arrive in the mail. Also cell phones worked all over the world, so it would not be nearly as difficult to stay in touch.

Gina thought her mother was going to tell her it would be best to end the relationship. Her support was unexpected. Her mother did bring up a valid point about communication being so much better than when she was her age. She could only imagine the anticipation and heartache of waiting every day to see if a letter would arrive in the mail. She was also surprised that her mother had confided in her about Charles. Ending her relationship with Charles must have broken her heart, and it was unfair for her grandparents to make her end the relationship. But it was a different time and place, and she was sure her grandparents thought they were doing what was best for her in the end.

Gina went to bed that night thinking of all her mother had said. She missed Damian so much that she had lost most of her appetite. It helped to keep busy, but she was surprised that it had been almost a week, and she still felt this way. She looked forward to his calls and loved to hear his voice. They never seemed to run out of things to talk about. Damian was intelligent, good looking, and he made her laugh. She knew it was too late. She had fallen in love with him. The only question that remained now was what to do about it.

The next day, she got up early as usual to start making breakfast for the guests. She was grateful that things were slow right now at the Inn. It made it easier since she still couldn't get around as fast since she hurt her ankle. It was healing, but it was taking longer than she would have liked. She was sad that her mom was leaving to go back to California, but she knew she needed to get back. She was grateful she was able to come and help out for as long as she did. She only wished she was going back with her, so she could see Damian.

She started the coffee and put the quiche in the oven that she had prepared the night before. Someone entered the kitchen, and she turned to see her mother. "You didn't have to get up so early." Gina sat out the plates and utensils.

"I know, but I wanted to spend some time with you before the guests got up." Her mom sat down on one of the bar stools. "I've enjoyed spending time with you, and I am really going to miss you. I want you to know that you do have options. If you wanted to move back to California, I'm sure your aunt and uncle could find someone else to run the Inn. Or they could come back and run it themselves. Please don't feel obligated to stay here if you are ready for your next adventure." Gina's mom smiled as she said it, but Gina knew she was serious.

Gina had been giving some serious thought to what she wanted to do next. The Inn had felt like home, but that was before she met Damian. Now she felt like wherever he was would be home. She realized now how military spouses did it. It was more about who you are with than where you lived or for how long. She was finally beginning to understand. Damian had offered to help her move to California. He said unless something unforeseen happened that he should be stationed in San Diego for at least three years. He had just finished his overseas tour, so he shouldn't have to go again for a while. At least he hoped not, and so did she.

She knew that her parents would be supportive of her decision, and now she had to decide what would be the right thing for her. She had considered applying for jobs in the San Diego area. She knew there were many resorts and B&Bs there, and with her experience she didn't think she would have a problem finding a job. At least she could live at the B&B, so she wouldn't have to pay rent since it was more expensive to live in California. She also didn't want to have a job that required her to work seven days a week, like she did now. She wanted to have some time off to spend with Damian since that would be the whole point of moving to California. She didn't know how she would break the news to her aunt and uncle. They had been traveling and enjoying their retirement, and she hated to ask them to find a replacement for her.

Then there was Vivian. She had become like family to her, and it would be difficult to leave her. She had considered asking Vivian if she would be interested in running the Blue Moon Inn. She thought that she would be an excellent replacement for her. She was not going to say anything to Vivian or her aunt and uncle until she was certain she was going to move.

She decided to send out a few resumes and see what happened. She didn't tell anyone her plans, not even Damian. But she knew with all her heart that her relationship with Damian was something special and extraordinary. She wasn't just going to walk away from it.

Chapter Twenty-Two

Kate was ecstatic to hear Frank's good news about the flower shop. She swore the baby moved at that exact moment, as if it agreed. She had talked to Matt about it and told him that she thought she was going to purchase the shop. She explained that she had reviewed the financials herself and also had them reviewed by an outside source and they both agreed it was a viable business decision. Matt was so surprised she could have knocked him over with a feather. He had let the issue go, thinking that Kate was just going to keep working at the bank. He took her out to dinner to celebrate. He had a glass of champagne and she had seltzer, but all in all it was a festive evening. She was meeting with the owner, her attorney, and her banker the next day to finalize the plans. Once they were finished she would let the bank know she would be leaving. She wanted to give them at least three weeks notice, as they had been good to her.

Things finally seemed to be going her way. One of the women she had talked to about babysitting once the baby was born was very interested in the position. She had given Kate her references and salary requirements, and Kate was going to check out her references as soon as she had the chance. She felt like her old self again, and it was wonderful.

Her mother had bought her some cute maternity clothes which she would need to be wearing very soon. She was not scheduled to see Dr. Yang again for another month, and so far the pregnancy was progressing well. The nausea had passed, and she was eating well. Every day she felt like the most blessed woman on the planet. She was making plans for some small changes at the flower shop, but didn't want to do anything major, at least not at first. The owner was pleased that Kate planned to keep the current help, as she knew the women enjoyed working there. Kate agreed and thought that was a wise decision. She knew those women would be teaching her the ropes, and they had a rapport with the current customers.

She had decided to wait until the baby was born to find out if it was a boy or girl, much to Matt's delight. As much as she wanted to know so she could plan the nursery, they decided to do it in pale shades of orange and blue. That way, no matter if it was a boy or girl, the colors would be fine. She had told her friends who wanted to give her a baby shower that they weren't finding out the sex of the baby. They were surprised, knowing what a planner Kate was, but seemed to take it in stride. They were not going to have the shower until her eighth month. By then Kate figured she would have things running smoothly at the flower shop and could concentrate on getting ready for the baby's arrival.

Things had improved slightly between her and Matt. He still seemed to be dealing with something, but, whatever it was, he didn't want to talk about it with her. She was trying to give him some space and figured he would talk to her when he was ready. He went out with his friends at least one night a week, and Kate wondered if that would continue after the baby was born. She didn't mind if he spent time with his friends, but things had changed lately. He would be vague about where he was going and would come in very late. She could smell alcohol on him, but he would say he only had a couple of drinks. She didn't want to fight with him about it. She figured maybe becoming a father was a little overwhelming, and he needed to feel like he could still have some fun. She truly thought that once the baby was born he would not go out as much.

They used to go out together and would often meet friends. But it seemed that in the past year Matt stopped asking her to go out with him and seemed to prefer to go out alone. She would get together with her friends over coffee a couple of times a month. She tried to tell herself that it was the same thing, but deep down she knew it wasn't. Somewhere in her heart she knew everything wasn't fine, but she thought with time maybe things would work out. Their lovemaking had become so infrequent; she couldn't remember the last time. *Maybe he is afraid it will hurt the baby. Maybe he just doesn't find me attractive anymore.* She wondered these things but she was just too afraid to ask him.

For now she focused on purchasing the flower shop and the baby. Her belly was growing, and she could feel the baby moving on a regular basis. She found herself talking and singing to it more and more often, especially now that she could feel it move. She could hardly believe that after all this time she was finally going to be a mom.

She had sent a fruit basket to Frank to thank him for reviewing the financial information she had sent him about the flower shop. She felt that was the least she could do. She thought she could manage the books herself, but had considered asking Frank to help with them after the baby was born. It would only be temporary, until the baby was a few months old and hopefully sleeping through the night. She hadn't officially asked him but was waiting to see how much work it would be once she got started. She might be able to handle it herself after all. In any case she was grateful to him for his help, and she had promised to keep in touch.

Frank was very surprised to receive the fruit basket at work. His co-workers teased him that he must have a secret admirer. He thought maybe it was from Maggie, and was surprised to read the card from Kate.

He smiled as he read the card, but his mind was on Maggie again. He had spoken to her on the phone earlier in the week, and she seemed distracted, to say the least. She said she would like to come to his place this weekend and maybe they could catch a movie and dinner. He wondered again if their relationship was ever going anywhere. Elaine, across the hall, had been very friendly lately, and he had considered asking her out. But if she was just recently separated from her husband, he didn't want to get into the middle of a possible reunion between them. He was smart enough to know that separations didn't always mean the relationship was over.

He put the fruit aside and picked up the phone. He dialed Kate's number but only reached her voice mail. He left her a nice message thanking her for the fruit basket and told her again she could call anytime if she needed his help.

Frank finished up the last minute details of an account before shutting down his computer. He felt tired to the bone. He had spent an enormous amount of energy thinking about Maggie and wondering where their relationship was headed. He finally decided that he was not going to worry about it anymore. If it worked out that was great, but if it didn't he would rather know sooner than later so he could get on with his life. He was going to stop trying so hard and just see where things went.

He wondered as he stepped on the elevator if his new way of thinking had anything to do with Elaine. It certainly helped his confidence to think there was another woman interested in him. *And not just any woman, but an intelligent, attractive woman*, he reminded himself. He drove the short distance home and stopped to get the mail on his way inside. Nothing exciting, just a few bills and a magazine. He hung up his coat and poured himself a drink. He didn't usually drink before dinner, but somehow he felt like he needed it tonight.

Frank was startled awake by the ringing of the telephone. He had dozed off after he finished his drink while sitting in his recliner. He was surprised to hear Maggie's voice.

"You sound a little sleepy, did I wake you?" Maggie asked as Frank tried to rub his handover his face in an attempt to wake up.

"No, not at all," Frank lied. "How are you?" he tried to change the subject.

"I've been better, but I'll survive," Maggie said in a sad tone.

"What's wrong?" Frank asked, suddenly concerned.

"Nothing I feel like discussing, at least not now. I was calling to see if I could come up earlier on Saturday. I thought maybe we could go out for lunch, and then to a vineyard up in the hills. There is one less than an hour from your house, and I thought that might be fun," Maggie said hopefully. She was really looking for a reason not to have to stay in her house, but she hoped she didn't sound desperate.

"That sounds fine. I didn't know you liked to go to vineyards," Frank said, wondering if she had told him that but he had forgotten.

"I've actually only been to one," Maggie admitted. "But I thought it might be fun to try something new together. I'll be there around noon then on Saturday," Maggie said.

"Sounds good to me," Frank said before saying good-bye.

Frank got up and made his way to the kitchen. He pulled out some leftover chicken from the refrigerator and put it on a plate. He had some salad, so he put the cold chicken on it and covered it with shredded cheese and dressing. He couldn't believe he had fallen asleep so quickly. Maybe he had been more stressed than he realized. He thought about the phone call from Maggie. She sounded down and not quite herself. He hoped she was fine. He had offered to talk about what was troubling her, but she obviously didn't want to discuss it. At least not with him.

After dinner he decided to shower and go to bed. Maybe a good night's sleep was what he needed. After climbing into bed he suddenly wasn't tired anymore. He lay staring up at the ceiling. He was thinking of Maggie and how much he liked her. She was a rare find, but he didn't know if she was willing to put her heart out there again. She had been crushed when Neal died, and he understood that. But it was as if he took her heart with him to the grave. Now if he could just figure out a way to resurrect it.

Chapter Twenty-Three

Damian had reported for duty at Camp Pendleton. He immediately liked the area. It was beautiful, close to the ocean, and had so much to do. There were surf shops on every block as he got closer to the beach. He was trying to check out some of the local restaurants so he could take Gina out if she ever came to visit. He thought eating outside while watching the sunset over the ocean would be very romantic.

He had put his things in his room and thought about calling Gina. He decided to call her later. He wanted to go explore the area. He got in his car and headed toward the beach. The sun was warm, and there was the smell of eucalyptus in the air. It wasn't humid like it had been on the East Coast. He drove along Highway 101, looking at the spectacular views of the ocean. He finally pulled into the parking lot of a small seafood restaurant that overlooked the bay. He went inside and was seated near a window. He could see surfers riding the waves in the distance. It was something he had always wanted to do, and now maybe he would have the chance to learn.

He ordered the fish taco special. He had never eaten one, but Gina said it was something he should try. He stared out at the crisp, blue water. The sun was dancing on the waves in the distance as a seagull swooped low to the water. He couldn't stop thinking about Gina. He missed her so much; he thought sometimes he wasn't going to make it through the day.

They had long talks every night on the phone, and he looked forward to that every day. But after they hung up, that emptiness crept back inside and he would lie in his bed thinking of her as he drifted off to sleep. He had never felt this way about a woman before, and he knew that this must be how love felt. He was still hoping Gina would move to California to be with him. He couldn't think of anything that would make him happier.

The waitress brought his food and it looked and smelled wonderful. It had fresh salsa with little bits of cilantro on it. After the first bite he knew he was hooked. Fish tacos were now a new favorite food. He wondered if Gina knew how to make them.

He watched the sun set over the ocean as he finished his dinner. He drove back to the base while listening to the oldies on the radio. He found himself talking out loud to his mother about Gina. He hoped it wasn't a sign that there was something wrong with him. It just made him feel closer to her somehow. He knew his mother would have liked Gina very much. He was hoping that the colonel would get to meet her soon. He was going to meet him tomorrow to have lunch and play a round of golf. He was grateful to be spending time with his father. He still couldn't bring himself to call him Dave, but maybe it would get easier if he spent more time with him out of uniform.

He called Gina at 9:00 o'clock most nights. By then she was finished with dinner and preparations for the next day's breakfast. Tonight he was excited to tell her about his fish taco dinner.

"I told you it was good!" Gina said with delight. "Whenever I visit we will have to go there for dinner. I haven't had a good fish taco in a while." Gina propped her ankle up on a stool. It was still painful by the end of the day, but it was slowly getting better.

"Is there any chance you can come out in the next couple of weeks?" Damian said hopefully. "I really miss you. In fact I feel like I'm going crazy sometimes without you."

Gina laughed. She felt the same way.

"I'm working on it," Gina said. She didn't tell him she had submitted her resume for some jobs in the area. She was hoping that she could come out for a job interview and visit him at the same time. She had made peace with the fact that the pace of life would be different in California. She knew it would be a faster pace, but she had hidden in the desert long enough. She missed being near the theaters and the ocean, and thought she would like living near San Diego. At least it wasn't Los Angeles, and she would still be close to her family.

They talked a little more before finally hanging up. Gina thought about Damian as she drifted off to sleep. But somewhere the dream turned into a nightmare. Visions of him leaving to go fight in a war swirled in her mind. She was crying, and he was trying to be brave. There were other people in uniform all around them, crying as the Marines had to board a plane. She suddenly was overcome with panic and fear that she would never see him again. She awoke with a start and sat up in bed. It took her a few moments to realize it was only a dream. After that, she couldn't sleep. She wondered if the dream was a sign of some sort. She prayed not.

Damian did not sleep well either. He was supposed to meet the colonel, his father, the next day to play a round of golf. He knew it was silly to be nervous, but that didn't change the fact that he was. He was grateful to have some family in his life, and looked forward to spending some time with Dave. Damian was trying to get used to calling him that, but somehow it just didn't seem to fit the man.

Damian had been thinking of Gina more and more and hoping that she would consider moving to California. He missed her more than he had imagined, and it left an ache inside him that never quite went away. He knew he was still grieving the loss of his mother, which was difficult. He had lost his mother, met his father that he previously hadn't known existed, met the love of his life, and transferred to a new duty station all in less than six months time. *No wonder I'm having trouble sleeping,* he thought when he considered all of the changes he had gone through in such a short amount of time. But he was a Marine, he reminded himself. Adapting and overcoming was something he had been trained to do. But he was realizing that adapting and overcoming was more difficult when it came to affairs of the heart.

Finally Damian put on headphones to listen to some music. Maybe that would help drown out the thoughts that were stealing his precious sleep.

Chapter Twenty-Four

Maggie couldn't wait to drive to Frank's house. She had not slept well since she had discovered Neal's affair, and she found it difficult to concentrate when she was at home. She wondered if she would ever feel the same way about the house. She had considered that perhaps their home was the place where he had been unfaithful, and the thought of it made her sick to her stomach. She had given it considerable thought and decided that it would have been nearly impossible as she was home all the time with Elizabeth, so there wouldn't have been much of an opportunity. Still she was restless and uneasy now when she was in the house. She felt like she wanted to run away but didn't know where to go. She had outbursts of anger that shocked her, and she was struggling to keep her emotions under control.

She had spoken to Elizabeth the night before and told her she was going on a date again with Frank.

Elizabeth grew quiet, and Maggie could sense that she wasn't totally comfortable with her dating again. She wondered if she thought dating was fine, but was worried it was growing more serious since they had been seeing each other for a few months now. She hoped that maybe she could meet Frank in the near future and that might change her mind.

Maggie sped along in her convertible with the top down; the wind rushing past her. She had tied a scarf around her hair before she left, so she wouldn't look totally unpresentable when she arrived at Frank's house. She had packed a picnic lunch for them as a surprise for Frank. She had been thinking more about him and decided she hadn't really given him much of a chance. She had been so busy comparing him to Neal that she had failed to see all of the good qualities about him. Today she was going to change that. Now she felt her eyes had been opened, and she was not feeling guilty in the least about spending time with Frank. In fact she was looking forward to it.

When the doorbell rang, Frank was combing his hair in the bathroom. He was wearing it a little shorter now and was trying to make an unruly piece of hair lay down. He rushed to the door and smiled broadly when he saw Maggie standing there. She wore a pair of white slacks and a blue top and looked absolutely stunning. She still had her scarf on her head and a pair of big sunglasses over her eyes. She looked like a movie star from the fifties, and Frank thought he had never seen any woman more beautiful.

Maggie reached up and kissed Frank lightly on the lips. He was pleasantly surprised. "How about we take my car," Maggie offered. "I packed a picnic lunch, and it is a great day to drive with the top down." Maggie smiled as she took off her sunglasses. Frank thought about his hair, so he grabbed a hat before heading out the door. Minutes later they were on their way to the vineyard.

As they drove along Frank noticed a seriousness about Maggie. He glimpsed some dark circles under her eyes when she had taken off her sunglasses but didn't say anything. Frank tried to make small talk, but it was hard to hear with the wind rushing past them. He finally gave up and on a whim decided to turn up the radio. A song he knew came blaring out of the speakers, and without thinking, Frank began to sing along. Maggie looked at him in surprise, but after a minute she joined in the song with him. By the time it was over they were both laughing so hard Maggie thought she was going to have to pull the car over.

When they arrived at the vineyard both of them were in good spirits. Frank took Maggie's hand as they headed inside. They toured the vineyard and tasted several good wines before they went out to retrieve the picnic basket from the car. Frank spread a blanket on the ground under a pine tree as Maggie began taking out the food she had prepared. There were sandwiches and fresh grapes along with sesame crackers and cheese. Maybe it was the wine but they were both feeling very relaxed and happy. Maggie realized she hadn't been this happy since before Neal had gotten ill. It felt so good to finally feel free and light again, even if only for a little while.

Over lunch, Frank told Maggie about talking with Kate West. He explained her idea of buying a flower shop and how he had looked over the financial reports for her. He told Maggie that Kate was expecting a baby and how happy she seemed. It was like talking to a different person. Kate had sent her regards to Maggie as well, which Maggie thought was kind. "Maybe that is why she seemed so sad when we were at the Blue Moon," Maggie said. "She was probably tired and fighting morning sickness." Maggie smiled as she began to gather up the remains of their lunch and put it back in the basket.

"I get the feeling that she didn't know she was pregnant at the time." Frank sighed as he rolled over on his back to look up at the sky. "Anyway, I'm really happy for her." He forced a smile. He was feeling a little sad that he would never have any children of his own.

As if reading his mind, Maggie asked, "Why didn't you have any children, if you don't mind my asking." Maggie stretched out beside Frank to gaze at the beautiful blue sky with him. There were only a few wispy clouds over head and there was the slightest hint of a breeze.

"I always wanted to have at least one child, maybe two. Carol just seemed to make excuses for why it was never the right time to have one. I honestly don't know if she really never wanted a child or if she just didn't want to have one with me," Frank said sadly. Maggie reached over and took his hand in hers and gave it a squeeze.

"Sometimes I wish that I had more children. Elizabeth was a bit of a surprise, so Neal was careful not to have any more surprises." Maggie brushed the hair away from her face. "Neal had a vasectomy when Elizabeth was eleven, so there wasn't any going back after that." Maggie remembered trying to convince Neal to wait, but he felt they couldn't afford another child and wanted to travel more instead.

"They say there is no perfect time to have a baby," Frank offered. "You know, you are not too old to have another one, women do it every day."

"I suppose not, but I don't know if I want to go through that all over again at my age. I guess I never considered it, really." Frank was surprised that she wasn't totally against the idea. But he knew how much she loved her daughter, and he could see her with a baby.

Maggie propped herself up on her elbow and looked down at Frank. He had a tiny scar on his chin that she hadn't noticed before. She reached down and kissed the scar, ever so gently. "Old war wound," Frank said. "I fell down and cut my chin when I was eight while my friend and I were playing like we were soldiers." Frank smiled and Maggie laughed. He was touched by her gesture and tenderness. He couldn't remember Carol ever noticing the scar before.

Frank took Maggie in his arms and kissed her. Gently at first but then with a hunger that came from deep inside. Maggie was breathless as he slowly released her. She was beginning to feel a stirring inside her, a longing to be with him more. After that they lay on the blanket and just held each other for a long time. Maybe it was the tenderness she felt but Maggie couldn't stop herself from crying. Frank didn't say anything but just held her and let her cry. He smoothed his hand over her hair and pulled her closer.

Finally Maggie sat up and reached for a tissue from her purse. She blew her nose and wiped her eyes and looked over at Frank. He didn't ask for an explanation, but she felt she owed him one. "Frank, I'm sorry," Maggie began. "You must think I'm ridiculous!" Maggie laughed as she said it, and Frank smiled.

"Not at all," Frank reassured her.

"I discovered something this week, and I am having a difficult time dealing with it." She paused as she gathered her courage. "I finally decided it was time for me to go through Neal's things and put some of them away." Maggie gazed out over the vineyard.

"That must have been very hard for you." Frank took her hand.

"It was. I was doing pretty well until I found a letter addressed to Neal. It was from a woman, one he obviously had an affair with earlier in our marriage." Maggie gasped as she tried to hold back the sob that managed to escape from her throat. A look of shock came over Frank.

"Oh, Maggie, I am so sorry." Frank put his arms around her. "Are you sure? Maybe it was just a woman who was infatuated with him," Frank said.

"No, I'm very sure. The worst part is Neal is not here to explain anything, and I feel guilty for being angry with a dead man," Maggie admitted. "I feel so betrayed, and it is even more unfair that I find out now when there is no way to get any answers." Maggie was trying not to cry again as she took a deep breath. "I'm just so angry. I don't know what to do. I don't even want to be in the house anymore," Maggie admitted to Frank.

"Does anyone else know that he had an affair? Is there anyone at all that might be able to fill in the blanks for you?" Frank asked. Maggie had not considered this before. She turned it over in her mind for a few moments, and all of sudden her eyes grew wide.

"I could ask his best friend, Adam. He's known Neal since grade school and if anyone would know, it would be him." Maggie turned toward Frank. "Thank you for suggesting that; it had never occurred to me before now. Maybe if I know the details I can come to grips with it," Maggie said. Frank thought that knowing the details might make it even more difficult, but he realized that men and women don't always think alike when it comes to matters of the heart.

Frank and Maggie spent the rest of the afternoon strolling around the area. They had bought some bottles of wine and browsed the local shops. Maggie liked that Frank didn't mind shopping and never complained about how long she took to look at things. Neither of them brought up Neal's affair again, but Maggie felt better after sharing the information with Frank. The more time she spent with him, the more she liked him. It was as if blinders had been lifted from her eyes, and she could see him more clearly. She did not feel guilty anymore about being with him and, in fact, was hoping she could spend a lot more time with him. She had the feeling that Frank was one of those men that you didn't let just pass through your life, he was one that was worth keeping.

They arrived back at Frank's house just as the sun was setting. He poured a glass of wine for each of them and invited Maggie out on the back patio to watch the sunset. It has been a wonderful day, and neither of them wanted to see it end. They sat in silence sipping their wine and holding hands. The sunset was gorgeous with hues of reds and oranges decorating the sky. As the sun went down, it got chilly, so they moved inside. Frank asked Maggie if she wanted to spend the night. He promised she could stay in the guest room, and he would try to control himself. Maggie considered it, as she wasn't eager to get back to her house. But she knew that they should not tempt themselves and that if Elizabeth called it would be difficult to explain.

After a tender kiss, Maggie hopped in her car and headed home. She put the top up since it had cooled off, and she sang along to the songs on the radio. She thought about Frank and the time they had shared. He was a remarkable and caring man, and she felt herself beginning to fall in love with him. She could sense that he wanted more from her, but was giving her time and space. She was grateful that he was so thoughtful and patient.

She was thinking back on the day, and what a nice time she had with Frank. For some reason her mind drifted to their conversation about having children. She could tell that Frank was very sad and disappointed that he did not have a child of his own. She thought it was a pity, because she knew that he would have been a wonderful father. She thought about his comment that she wasn't too old to have a baby. She would be forty next year, but she knew women who had children later in life. Suddenly thinking of having another child didn't seem so strange; she kind of liked the idea. She wasn't sure what Elizabeth would think. Probably that she had gone stark raving mad.

As she rounded the corner to her house, she pushed the thoughts out of her mind. When she looked at the house she suddenly had the urge to keep driving. She knew she couldn't run away from this; she was going to have to work through it. She turned the key in the door and turned on the light. Maybe after a hot shower she would feel better.

She had decided to call Adam the next day. Whatever skeletons were in the closet needed to come out now, so that she could have some closure. She felt she deserved an explanation, even if Neal wasn't there to give her one. She only hoped she could convince Adam of it.

Maggie was up early and drinking her second cup of coffee when the phone rang. It was Frank, asking if she made it home safely. She was touched by his concern. Frank offered to go with her to talk to Adam, but Maggie insisted this was something she needed to do alone. Besides, she wasn't sure how open Adam would be with Frank there, and she wanted all the details. They made plans to see each other the next weekend. This time Frank said he would drive to her place and maybe they could rent some movies, and he would make her dinner. Maggie was hoping Elizabeth would come home for the weekend. She thought it was time she met Frank. He promised to call later in the week, and she knew that he would. She also knew that if she needed him, he would be there. It was strange to think she could depend on someone again, but it felt good not to feel so alone.

After eating half a bagel and cream cheese, Maggie took a deep breath and picked up the phone. She dialed Adam's number, and he answered on the second ring. "Maggie, it's so good to hear from you. How are you?" Maggie fidgeted with her hair. Adam had been a good friend to Neal and she genuinely liked him. He and his wife had divorced about five years ago, and he now had a serious girlfriend. She had a feeling they would eventually get married, but Adam was a little more cautious this time. He had two wonderful daughters that he spent a large amount of time with, and he was in no hurry to tie the knot.

"I'm fine, Adam. How are you?" Maggie said, trying to make small talk.

"I can't complain. The girls are growing like weeds and I haven't been overwhelmed by estrogen yet."

Maggie laughed. She knew his girls were fifteen and thirteen and remembered how hard those years had been with Elizabeth. Maggie decided to get to the point.

"Adam, I was wondering if maybe you could meet me for coffee sometime today. I know it is short notice, but I really need to talk with you." Maggie tried not to sound as desperate as she felt.

"Sure. I have to drop the girls off around three, so I could meet you at the café on the corner of Fifth street around three-thirty." Adam sounded a little alarmed. "Is everything all right?" he asked.

"Yes, I just need to get some answers and you are the only one who might have them," Maggie said. "I'll meet you at three-thirty." Maggie hung up before he could ask her any more questions. There were just some things that needed to be done face to face and this was one of them.

Maggie tried to keep busy, but her mind would not stay focused. She had tucked the letter she found in her purse to show Adam. She did a load of laundry and a little cleaning. She knew she needed to get started on an article for a magazine she was working for, but she just couldn't concentrate right now. Finally it was time for her to meet Adam. She couldn't believe how nervous she felt. She wondered if she really wanted the truth, and what it would change even if she knew. But, somehow she had to know and wouldn't rest until she had all the answers.

When Adam came into the café, Maggie was already sitting in a booth near the back. She got up to hug him and told him she had ordered a latte for both of them. Adam knew by looking at her that something was making her very nervous. She looked tired and had dark circles under her eyes. She had her hair pulled back which made her look more serious than usual and a silk scarf around her neck. He had always thought she was very pretty but somehow couldn't bring himself to ask her out on a date after Neal died. He would have felt like he had betrayed his best friend. He had been there for both of them through Neal's battle with cancer and was there for her if she needed him now. At first she called him more frequently, but with time she adjusted to life on her own.

Adam took her hand across the table. "Look, Maggie, I've known you long enough to know that there is something up, so cut to the chase and just tell me what is going on." Maggie raised her eyes to meet his. She took the letter out of her purse and handed it to him.

"I found this when I was going through Neal's things. I need some answers, Adam. I deserve that, especially now. Please, you have to be honest with me. Don't try to lie to protect Neal or me. I need to know all the details, or I'm never going to be able to get past this and have some peace." Maggie's eyes pleaded with Adam. He knew without even reading the letter that Maggie had found out the one thing that Neal feared the most. "I'm not even going to be angry with you for not telling me before now because I know how close you and Neal were. I just need you to be honest with me now. Please, Adam, that's not too much to ask." Maggie wiped away a tear from her cheek, slightly embarrassed.

Adam took the letter from her trembling hand and read it. It made him feel sick reading the faded words. He had known about Neal's affair and had been sworn to secrecy. But now that Maggie had proof, he just couldn't keep quiet any longer. Neal should have told her himself a long time ago. He had tried to convince Neal to tell her, that they could work things out, but he refused. He felt that Maggie would leave him, and he didn't want to take that chance. He ended the affair and took his secret to the grave.

Adam sat the letter down and looked Maggie in the eye. "I'm not going to lie to you, Maggie. The letter is true. Neal had an affair. I'm not going to make excuses for him, because it was wrong, and I know he regretted it the rest of his life," Adam said hoping to make her feel a little better.

"I want details, Adam. Who was she, why did he do it? Were there others? Why didn't he tell me?" Maggie began firing questions at Adam.

"Slow down. I'll do my best to recall as much as I can. But you have to remember it was a long time ago." Adam squeezed her hand.

Adam took a deep breath. "Neal met this woman at a bar one night. He had been really stressed with work, finances, and the fact that he was about to become a father. Don't get me wrong, he adored Elizabeth, but at the time he was so young, and the pregnancy wasn't planned. He was overwhelmed with the responsibility of it all. You know as well as I do that Neal was more like a boy sometimes than a man." Adam laughed as Maggie shook her head in agreement. "Anyway we were shooting some pool, and this woman kept flirting with Neal. She just wouldn't leave him alone. He thought it would be fun to just flirt back, but things got a little out of hand." Adam looked away as he took a sip of his latte while trying to decide the best way to tell her the rest of the story.

"Neal ended up leaving the bar with this woman, even though I tried my best to talk him out of it. He saw her almost every day for two weeks." Adam stopped to let Maggie absorb this news, as he knew it was not easy for her to hear that. "At first, I think he thought it would be just some harmless flirting. But when you mix stress, frustration, alcohol, and a willing woman together the result is disastrous." Adam looked away from Maggie; he couldn't stand to see the pain in her eyes. "After Elizabeth was born, he tried to break things off with her, but she was persistent. She tried to convince him to leave you, that she was the only one for him. Finally he knew he was in too deep. He was very afraid that you would find out and leave him. Despite his faults, Neal loved you, and I know he never meant to hurt you. He ended the affair and swore me to secrecy. His biggest fear was that you would find out," Adam sighed.

"Then why did he keep this letter from her all these years?" Maggie asked.

"I don't know. But you know that Neal was not organized at all, and most likely shoved it in the back of the closet and thought he would deal with it later. Maybe you came home just as he was reading it, and he stashed it away and forgot about it." Maggie knew Neal was not one to go through things in his closet, or any other room. Neatness was never something Neal ascribed to.

"What did she look like?" Maggie asked quietly. She had to know all the details now.

"Gee, Maggie, you must think I have a great memory," Adam laughed. He remembered very well what she looked like but wanted to spare Maggie the details.

"Tell me what you remember," Maggie persisted.

"She was not bad looking. Tall, dark hair, small boned. Worked at another bar, if I remember correctly." Adam swallowed hard. He hoped the details he told her were enough to satisfy her curiosity. He didn't want to tell her that this woman was beautiful. She had olive colored skin and looked very exotic. She wore low cut tops, tight skirts, and her hair was long and silky and flowed over her shoulders. She had a great figure and was the kind of woman that turned heads. He knew why Neal was attracted to her because every man in the bar that night was too. Why she zeroed in on Neal, he never knew. Maybe it was his outgoing personality and his boyish good looks. She could have had her choice of men, but she picked Neal. Unfortunately he didn't have sense enough to walk away.

"Why didn't he tell me? How could he have lived with the guilt all those years?" Maggie asked as she took a sip of her latte, which had gone cold.

"He vowed to make it up to you. He really thought if you knew he would lose you, and he just couldn't stand the thought of that. He felt the guilt was his punishment and that you should not have to be hurt for his actions," Adam said quietly.

"Were there other women?" Maggie narrowed her eyes. She had to have the whole truth now.

"No, there weren't. Neal had his faults, but he loved you. You are just going to have to trust that he never meant to hurt you. He made a mistake, a huge one. But you have to know in your heart, that he really loved and cared about you and Elizabeth."

Maggie's anger had eased some. She remembered what a stressful time it was when she was pregnant with Elizabeth. They barely made ends meet, and they blamed each other. They were very young, and just starting out. Having a baby meant putting their dreams on hold and that went against everything that Neal had wanted. He had been a wonderful father, and she was grateful that he wasn't resentful toward Elizabeth.

Maggie smiled at Adam. "Are there any other deep dark secrets you think I should know?" Adam returned the smile.

"No, there isn't. And for what it's worth, it pained me greatly to keep this from you all these years. I was kind of stuck between a rock and a hard place, if you know what I mean." He squeezed Maggie's hand. For all she had been through, her eyes were still bright and blue.

"Thank you, Adam. I know this may sound strange, but I feel better somehow." Maggie took the last sip of her latte and got up to leave. Adam paid the check and walked her to her car. Maggie hugged Adam and kissed his cheek. "Thank you again. I appreciate your honesty, even if it is almost twenty years late." She smiled and he hugged her again. Adam promised he would be in touch and told her to call if she needed anything. "Tell the girls hello for me," she called as she walked to her car.

Maggie felt more peaceful on the drive home. At least now she knew the truth. After thinking back to that time in their life, she thought about how Neal must have felt. He was so young, with a wife and an unexpected baby on the way. Finances were tight, and they were fighting constantly. Neal felt like his youth was being snatched away, and his dreams put on hold. Maggie had felt that way too, but she was also excited about becoming a mother. She was always the more responsible one in their relationship she realized now. Maggie reached over and turned the radio off.

"I forgive you, Neal," she said out loud. "I'm not saying what you did was right, but I understand. I wish you would have told me when you were alive," Maggie sobbed. But after thinking about it, she wondered if she really wished that. Was Neal right in assuming she would leave him? If she had, Elizabeth would have had a very different childhood. Would she have been able to forgive him and stay in their marriage? She didn't really know what she would have done. Maggie decided she couldn't turn back the clock, so the only choice was to forgive Neal and move forward. She needed to do that, not for him, but for herself.

Chapter Twenty-Five

Kate was having the time of her life. She had purchased the flower shop and was enjoying going to work every day. Business was good, and she was learning fast. She liked both of the ladies that worked for her and was grateful they stayed on once she bought the shop. The morning sickness was gone, and she was safely in her second trimester. She was wearing maternity clothes now and could feel the baby moving on a regular basis. Matt had been spending a little more time at home lately, much to her delight.

Kate couldn't believe how just a few months had changed everything. She felt like her old self again. She had more energy and was hopeful for the first time in a long time. She even found a part-time nanny that she liked and wanted to hire after the baby was born.

Kate was trying to get Matt to help decorate the nursery, but somehow he kept putting it off. He always seemed to have something else to do whenever she brought up the subject. She decided she would give him one last chance, and, if he didn't help her, she was going to ask her mom. She was trying not to be too pushy with Matt; she still didn't feel like their marriage was on solid ground. She still saw her therapist from time to time, but she felt like she was doing pretty well now. Matt refused to go with her, claiming there was nothing wrong with him. Her therapist cautioned her that she didn't think having a baby would solve all of her problems, but could in fact create some new ones, especially in her marriage.

Matt pretended everything was fine until she started talking about the baby or the nursery. He kept asking her what her hurry was; she still had months to go until the baby arrived. He didn't even want to discuss names for the baby. Kate was beginning to wonder if he really wanted a baby after all. She had read that often this was a difficult transition for men to make, so she was trying to give him some time. She just didn't want to be raising this child alone. She thought Matt would be a great dad once the baby arrived and was hoping that with time he would be more excited.

Kate called Gina at least once a week. They had become good friends, and she looked forward to their conversations. Gina always seemed to bring a fresh perspective to things, and she appreciated her honesty. She had encouraged Gina to look for a job in California in order to be closer to Damian. She had even called one of her friends from college who lived near

San Diego to see if she needed anyone in her catering business. Fran had been running her own catering business since college, and Kate had kept in touch over the years. Fran was thrilled to hear Kate was expecting and told her she was still looking for Mr. Right.

Fran told Kate that she might have an opening soon, as one of her employees was moving because her husband was being transferred. She promised to call if she did, and said she would be glad to interview Gina. Kate had not shared this news with Gina because she didn't want to get her hopes up. She knew Gina would be great for the job and only hoped Fran would call her soon. She didn't know how much longer Gina could stand being apart from Damian.

Kate thought back to when she and Matt were that in love. They had met her sophomore year of college. He sat behind her in biology class, and every day, as he walked past, he smiled but didn't say anything. Finally, as the semester was about to end, he got up the nerve to ask her to a party. They had a great time and talked for hours. After that they were inseparable. Six months after graduation they got married and bought their house. She still loved Matt very much; they had just hit a bump in the road of marriage, that's all. At least that is what Kate told herself. She couldn't quite put her finger on it, but deep down she knew something didn't feel the same with Matt. But everything else in her life was going so well— she didn't let herself dwell on it.

Kate had teased Gina that when she and Damian got married, she was going to do the flowers for the wedding. Gina laughed and told her she thought she was getting ahead of herself. But Kate knew that Gina and Damian were crazy about each other. Even if Gina had her reservations about being a Marine's wife, she thought that she would see in the end that the sacrifice was worth it.

Kate made her way to the flower shop. She liked to be the first one there to open up in the mornings, even though Helen had a key. She liked Helen, and she had helped her learn more about the business. She was a grandmother and talked about her family often. Helen was excited that Kate would be bringing the baby into the shop after it was born. She hoped that it would not be too much of a distraction for either of them, so that it affected their work. Helen was not the fastest at arranging flowers, but her arrangements were beautiful and unique. Jody worked only three afternoons a week unless Kate needed her to make extra deliveries. She was quiet and reserved but was warming up to Kate. She was always on time and did whatever Kate asked of her. She got the feeling that Jody had a difficult time trusting others, and that perhaps she had been mistreated in her life. Jody didn't talk much about her personal life, and Kate didn't want to pry. She figured with time maybe she would feel like sharing some of the details of her life with her.

When Kate opened the door the phone was already ringing. She rushed to answer it and began writing down the order. Business had been good, and she had made a profit the first month. It wasn't quite as much as she had made at the bank, but it was a decent amount, and Kate was satisfied with that.

A few minutes later Helen came in the door wearing a big straw hat. She liked to walk to work if the weather was nice, and she was meticulous about sun protection. It definitely showed. She had porcelain skin and very few wrinkles. She really didn't look her age at all, and Kate felt guilty for not taking better care of her skin. She was trying to use all the right lotions and creams so as not to get stretch marks, and so far it seemed to be working.

Kate and Helen worked side by side all morning. She enjoyed talking with Helen in between customers. She was surprised when she looked up and saw Matt coming in the door.

"Hi, I'd like to speak to the owner of the shop," Matt said to Kate. Kate decided to play along.

"Is there a problem, sir?" Kate tried to look serious as she looked at Matt.

"Yes, there is. I would like to take the owner to lunch, if she is available." Matt smiled at Kate and made her heart melt.

"I think that can be arranged." Kate slid her work apron off.

Kate introduced Matt to Helen and then told her she was going to lunch. Helen was capable of managing the shop alone for a couple of hours and told her to go and have a good time. "So what's the occasion?" Kate asked as they walked to a nearby café.

"Does there have to be a reason for everything?" Matt snapped. Kate was stung by his words. Matt looked nervous as they stepped onto the side street. They walked in silence the rest of the way.

They made small talk over lunch. When they had finished eating, Matt grew serious. She thought he had seemed nervous throughout the meal, but the look on his face told her that whatever he was about to say was going to be something she didn't want to hear.

"Katie, I don't know any other way to say this. No matter what I do, there is no easy way to say what I have to say." Kate sat perfectly still staring Matt in the eye. The baby inside her moved, as if it knew this was not going to be good news.

Matt continued, "These past couple of years has been really hard for both of us. But it has made me realize that we want very different things. You want a baby and a family man. You wanted that above everything else, including me."

Kate opened her mouth to protest, but Matt held up his hand. "Let me finish."

Kate leaned back in her chair and took a sip of water, as her mouth had gone dry.

"In the beginning, I wanted a baby too. But when it didn't happen for so long, I began to feel like you would never be happy with just me. You became so obsessed with having a baby that our marriage didn't matter to you anymore. I felt like I was just a tool you were using to get what you wanted." Matt looked away from Kate's glare, as he gathered the courage to continue.

"Somewhere along the line, I fell out of love with you. You became someone I didn't recognize anymore. I have tried my best to make it work, but I just can't pretend that I love you anymore when I don't. It isn't fair to you, me, or our child to continue this charade any longer. We each need to be free to try and move on with our lives. I will be a father to our baby, but I just can't be your husband anymore." Matt sighed with relief that he had finally said what was on his mind.

Kate felt like a boulder had landed on her heart. She knew things had not been good between them, but she never expected Matt to leave her. "Your timing is great, as usual," Kate hissed in an undertone.

"I was planning to tell you when you returned from New Mexico, but then you came home and told me you were pregnant, so I decided to stay and try and make it work. But, I'm sorry, I just can't go through the motions anymore. You can stay in the house, and I promise I will pay child support."

"I bet you were hoping all along, that I would lose this baby, and then you could wash your hands of me without any guilt!"

"That is not true!" Matt raised his voice and people turned to look at them.

"I think you are selfish! You aren't worried about how this will affect our child! You are a quitter! You wouldn't even go to counseling with me, so that we could try and work things out. You just want to throw in the towel because it isn't what you want anymore." Kate didn't care who was looking at them now.

Kate got up from her chair and picked up her bag. With a backward glance she said through gritted teeth, "My attorney will be in touch."

On the way back to the flower shop, Kate began to feel a cramping pain in her abdomen. It subsided after a few minutes, but then it would begin again. *Probably just growing pains*. "Don't worry little baby, no matter happens, I will take good care of you." Kate cooed softly as she rubbed her growing belly. She only hoped that was true.

Kate went back inside the shop, her mind spinning. She threw herself into work so she wouldn't have to think about how her life was falling apart…again. She knew that Matt would be gone when she got home and that she would have plenty of time to think about what she was going to do next. Just then her cell phone rang, and Kate reached in her purse to grab it. It was Fran.

She wanted to let Kate know that her employee was in fact moving and she was hoping she could get Gina's phone number. Kate tried to sound excited. She gave Fran Gina's number but asked her to wait ten minutes before she called. She wanted to call her first to let her know Fran would be calling to discuss the position, so she could be prepared. Fran agreed and thanked Kate before hanging up.

Gina rushed inside to answer the phone. She had been watering the flowers in front of the Inn, and had forgotten to take the cordless phone with her.

"Hello," Gina said breathlessly.

"Hi, Gina, it's Kate. You sound out of breath." Kate pulled some yellow roses from the refrigerator.

"I was outside watering the flowers, and I forgot to take the cordless with me," Gina explained. "How are you?" Gina asked.

Kate fought back the tears. She refused to cry at work. She forced a smile before replying.

"I'm great." She hated to lie, but she just couldn't talk about it right now. Her emotions were too raw. "I have some good news for you." Kate tried to sound excited.

"Go on," Gina said wondering what good news she could possibly have for her.

"I just spoke to a friend of mine named Fran. We've been good friends since college. She runs a catering business near San Diego, and she is needing to hire someone. I gave her your number and she is going to be calling you in about five minutes." Gina was speechless.

"Gina, are you there? Did you hear what I said?" Kate asked. She hoped she hadn't overstepped her boundary by giving Fran Gina's number.

"Yes, I heard you. I just can't believe it! I was just applying for more jobs this morning online. The timing couldn't be better." Gina was smiling as she wiped her hair from her eyes.

"Fran started her company from the ground up right out of college. She is honest, fair, and organized. I think it would be a good fit. Of course, I told her you came highly recommended." Kate laughed, and so did Gina.

"Thank you, Kate. I really mean it. My aunt called this morning and said that she and my uncle were finally tired of traveling. It seems my uncle is suffering from gout and arthritis, and it is getting too hard for them to travel all the time. Anyway, she said they are moving back to the Inn. They should be here in a week or two." Gina sat down on a barstool in the kitchen.

"Then it was meant to be," Kate said as a matter of fact. "Now, we better hang up, so Fran can get through to you. Let me know how it goes." Gina promised she would and after thanking Kate again she hung up the phone.

Gina sat there, hardly believing what had happened. She tried to clear her mind so she would be ready when Fran called. She knew Damian would be so excited if she got a job near him, so they could be together. She had butterflies in her stomach just thinking about him. Just then, the phone rang again. Gina took a deep breath and hoped that this would be the call that changed everything for the better.

Gina and Fran talked for nearly an hour. Fran needed a catering director and was impressed by Gina's education and experience. She explained the company's philosophy and the job in detail. It sounded wonderful to Gina. Gina told her she could start in three weeks, which would be perfect Fran said. Fran asked her to email her a copy of her resume and references, and if everything checked out the job was hers. Gina offered to come to San Diego for an interview, but Fran said she had basically done the interview over the phone.

She said if Kate recommended her then she trusted her judgment.

When Gina hung up the phone, she started jumping up and down. Vivian walked into the kitchen and began laughing.

"Why are you so excited?" Vivian asked as she sat down two bags of groceries.

"I was just offered a job in San Diego. And not just any job, but as catering director for an established catering company." Gina was smiling, but the look on Vivian's face told her she was not as happy about the news.

"That's great, I guess. When will you be leaving?" Vivian avoided looking at Gina as she put the groceries away.

"Vivian, I will miss you so much. But my aunt and uncle are coming back to run the Inn. Apparently my uncle has gout and arthritis, and they just aren't able to travel much now. My aunt just called this morning, so I didn't get a chance to tell you. I already talked to her, and she definitely wants you to continue working here. You will like her, I promise," Gina said hopefully. Vivian sat down on a bar stool. She was a little overwhelmed with all of the changes. "I know it is a lot to absorb, but please try and be happy for me," Gina pleaded. "There wouldn't be a place for me here with my aunt and uncle returning, and you know how I feel about Damian. Besides I won't be so far away that we can't ever visit each other," Gina said hopefully.

"I know, but things won't be the same. My grandmother will miss you too." Vivian looked like she might cry.

"I'll miss you both and the Inn. But I feel like the time has come for me to move on. You know how much I love to cook, and now my education will be put to good use." Gina put an arm around Vivian's shoulder. "I'm counting on you to keep this place running smoothly. I have a feeling my aunt has forgotten how much work this place can be."

Gina sat down next to Vivian. She poured them each a glass of lemonade and then made a toast to the future. She promised Vivian they would have a girl's night out before she left. "Besides you will probably be settling down one day," Gina said. Vivian had been seeing Jack Hayfield for nearly two years. Everyone knew Jack would marry Vivian in a minute if only she would agree to it. She said she was waiting until they had enough money saved to buy a place of their own. She didn't want to live with her grandmother or Jack's family. That was no way to start a marriage. Gina never thought Jack was her type, but she had kept her opinion to herself.

Gina helped Vivian finish putting away the groceries before starting dinner. She could hardly wait to tell Damian the news. She decided to wait and call him later when she could talk privately in her room. There were still some details she wanted to work out in her mind before telling him. She went to the computer and sent her resume and references to Fran. She was excited about starting a new chapter of her life.

Gina made enchiladas for dinner with Spanish rice. The guests raved about her cooking, which made her glad that she was going to get to continue her passion. Finally the dishes were done and the kitchen clean. She had prepared the breakfast casserole she was serving in the morning, so everything was in place. After a check on the guests out on the patio she finally escaped to her room to call Damian. She decided to wait and call Kate tomorrow. Knowing Kate she probably already spoke to Fran and knew all the details anyway.

Her hands trembled as she dialed his number. After the third ring he finally answered. "Hi, Damian, it's Gina." She took a deep breath.

"How are you?" he asked.

"Wonderful!" Gina tossed her long hair over her shoulder.

"How can you be wonderful, if you're not with me?" Damian teased.

"What if I told you all that was about to change? I got a job in the San Diego area. I start in three weeks." Gina bounced up and down on the bed. Damian let out a loud whoop. He asked her all about the job, and she filled him in on all the details.

"You have made me one of the happiest men alive," Damian said. He couldn't believe she was finally going to be moving to California to be with him.

Gina asked Damian if he would find an apartment for her. He was surprised she trusted him that much.

She explained that her aunt and uncle were returning and that she needed to stay at the Inn and get things in order. She also told him that she didn't really have much furniture, so they would have to go shopping once she got there. Damian knew already that he was going to try and find a place about half way between where she worked and Camp Pendleton. There were lots of apartments in the area, so he knew he shouldn't have too much difficulty finding one. He just hoped it would be something she liked. He quizzed her about her likes and dislikes when it came to housing, so he could be sure and rent something suitable.

They talked for over an hour, making plans and finalizing details. After he hung up Damian was so excited he needed to tell someone his good news. He picked up the phone and called the colonel. When he told him Gina got a job and was moving to California, his father was happy for him. He told Damian he definitely wanted to meet this woman that was going to be his future daughter-in-law.

"How can you be so sure of that?" Damian asked.

"Because I know a man in love when I see one," said the colonel. Damian thought about what his father had said after they hung up. He made up his mind and knew what he had to do.

Kate locked up the shop and headed home. She was drained and wanted nothing more than a hot bath and a bite to eat. She grabbed the mail on her way into the house and made her way to the kitchen. Matt was nowhere to be found, but she didn't expect he would be. After eating a bowl of soup and a sandwich, Kate went to run a bath.

As Kate began undressing she suddenly looked down in horror. She couldn't believe her eyes. There was bright red blood trickling down her leg. She immediately called her mother and asked her to take her to the emergency room. She didn't want to explain why Matt couldn't take her to the hospital, so she told her mom he was working late.

Kate sat on the edge of the tub and took a deep breath. She was trying hard not to panic. She contemplated calling Matt, but decided that if didn't love her anymore, then he probably wouldn't care what happened to her. The more she thought about it, the more she convinced herself that it was his fault this was happening to her and their baby. If he hadn't upset her so, she probably wouldn't be dealing with this right now. She fought back the sobs, as she said a prayer that her baby would survive.

Chapter Twenty-Six

Maggie was nervous about Frank meeting Elizabeth. She was pleased that Elizabeth was making an effort to be open-minded about her dating. She had matured considerably since starting college. Maggie assured Frank that everything would be fine, but she wasn't entirely convinced of it herself. They had decided to meet at a restaurant in town while Elizabeth was home from college. Maggie thought that would be more neutral ground, rather than having Elizabeth meet Frank at home. Frank had agreed.

Frank changed his clothes twice before deciding on gray pants and a blue blazer. He had researched the college Elizabeth was attending, so he could make small talk about that. He thought about bringing her and Maggie some flowers, but decided against it. He knew that Maggie's feelings for him had grown, and that it was an important next step for him to meet her daughter. Maggie had described her as feisty and stubborn, but said she had a huge heart and was very involved in volunteering opportunities on campus. He hoped and prayed that she liked him, because he knew it would be difficult for Maggie if she didn't.

Frank was already seated at the restaurant when Maggie and Elizabeth arrived. He had learned that Maggie was usually a little late, so he wasn't surprised to have arrived first. After the introductions they all sat down and began looking at the menu. Elizabeth was tall, with dark hair and Maggie's blue eyes. She was a pretty girl, but he could tell that she was guarded around him.

After they ordered, Frank asked Elizabeth about college. She was impressed that he knew so much about her school. Maggie was touched that Frank had taken the time to do some research. She knew how nervous he was to meet Elizabeth and how much he wanted her to like him. She wanted Elizabeth to like Frank too, because somehow, she needed her approval.

After a while Elizabeth seemed to relax a little. They talked about sports, which impressed Frank very much. She was quite a baseball fan, and they talked for a long time about their favorite teams. They enjoyed a nice dinner, and all in all it turned out to be a nice evening. Frank paid the check, and Maggie told Elizabeth that Frank would bring her home. "Don't stay out too late," Elizabeth teased. Maggie hugged her daughter before she left the restaurant. She was relieved that they seemed to like each other.

Maggie and Frank decided to walk to a nearby park. It was a beautiful evening, and the air was fresh with the scent of flowers and freshly cut grass. They took a seat on a bench overlooking a small lake. Children were playing tag by the last light of day. Frank took Maggie's hand and turned to look at her. He still couldn't believe how fortunate he was to have found her. Maggie reached up and kissed him. It was a tender, slow kiss full of all the emotions that she had been feeling.

They talked about the evening, and Frank told her he thought Elizabeth was an intelligent and wonderful young woman. He could see why she was so proud of her. Maggie was glad they liked each other. She thanked Frank for taking the time to make such an effort with Elizabeth. It really touched her that he thought it was so important.

It was getting cooler, so they walked the two blocks back to Frank's car. He hated for the evening to end, but he knew Maggie wanted to spend some time with Elizabeth since she was home for the weekend. He drove her home but decided not to come inside. He promised to call in the next few days, and she knew he would. If there was one thing she knew about Frank, it was that he kept his word. He kissed her softly and held her an extra minute. In her soul she felt like she had come home being in his arms. She no longer felt guilty for being with him. In a strange way finding out about Neal's affair had freed her to move forward with her life. Fate had a way of working things out she decided.

Maggie found Elizabeth reading her email when she walked into the living room. She smiled at her daughter and squeezed her shoulders.

"I really like Frank." Elizabeth hit the send button on her computer. "It seems a little strange to see you with someone other than Dad, but I know you don't need to be alone forever." She turned and got up from her chair to hug her mom. Maggie was surprised to find she had tears streaming down her cheeks.

"I'm so glad you like Frank, because I really like him too." Maggie reached for a tissue.

"I could tell you two are kind of serious about each other, otherwise I don't think Frank would have been so nervous, and you wouldn't have bothered to introduce us," Elizabeth said with a laugh.

"We've never really talked about it, but, yes, I think we both feel like this could be a more permanent relationship." Maggie smiled as she thought about being with Frank for the rest of her life.

"Maybe I'll finally get that brother or sister I always wanted!" Elizabeth teased.

Maggie rolled her eyes. "Be careful what you wish for."

Maggie and Elizabeth spent the rest of the weekend watching old movies and eating pizza at home. She was reminded of how grown-up Elizabeth had become and how she was a woman now. She thought the years had gone by too fast but was immensely proud of the person Elizabeth had grown to be. She thought of Neal and how proud he would be of her too. The anger she had toward Neal had turned into acceptance. The good far outweighed the bad in their marriage, and she was not going to hold onto the anger any longer. She never mentioned the letter she had found to Elizabeth, as she knew how much she adored her father. It served no purpose in her life to know about his affair because that was between her and Neal.

After Elizabeth went back to college, Maggie was suddenly inspired to start on a new writing assignment. She felt hopeful again and somehow more peaceful than she had been since Neal passed away. After cleaning out Neal's things she had bought a new bedspread and curtains, and she liked the new look of her bedroom. She even rearranged the furniture, so the space felt different to her now.

Frank called her almost every night and they talked for hours. They both looked forward to talking to each other every day. Frank said that he had heard from Kate West, that Gina was moving to California to be closer to her boyfriend, Damian. She was starting a new catering job near San Diego, which they both agreed was a wonderful idea. He told her Gina's aunt and uncle had returned to run the Inn, so it worked out well. Kate's flower shop was doing well, and Frank was glad to hear it. He would have felt bad if the business had been a flop, after he recommended she buy the shop. Frank asked Maggie if she ever thought about going back to the Blue Moon Inn, only this time with him. Maggie wondered if it would be the same with Gina gone, and Frank agreed. They decided to wait and see how things went, and then possibly take a trip in the fall to New Mexico.

Frank was working hard but enjoying his work. Elaine was still coming by his office to chat but less frequently now. He tried not to encourage her but was amused by her excuses to talk with him. He had heard that she was dating someone in the mail room, and he was relieved. She was a pretty woman but not one that he could see himself with long-term. She liked to dress provocatively and pushed the limits when it came to the company dress code. Although she was nice to look at, he knew that a woman like that could be trouble.

He turned his thoughts to Maggie, and found himself smiling. He was in love with her and had told her so over the weekend. They had been walking in the park when he stopped and turned to kiss her ever so gently. He was pleased when she told him she loved him in return. Ever since then he had felt like he was walking on air. He could see a future with her, and they had briefly talked about it on the phone the night before. Just the fact that she was open to the possibility to spending the rest of their lives together was a huge step in the right direction as far as Frank was concerned.

Frank realized that he no longer heard Carol's voice in his mind throughout the day. It had been replaced with thoughts of Maggie. He had heard from a mutual friend, that Carol had married a much younger man, and that she was expecting a baby. He had gone to a bar to try and ease the pain of it the day he found out, but it still nagged him. He now knew for certain that it wasn't the fact that Carol didn't want children; she just didn't want to have his. Somehow that hurt more than he expected.

He tried to console himself with the thought that if he and Maggie got married he would have Elizabeth as a stepdaughter. But he knew it wasn't the same thing as she was a grown woman now. His mother had been so disappointed that he had not given her grandchildren before she died. But the past was the past he reminded himself, and he felt blessed to have found Maggie. She was everything he wanted and more, and he was already thinking of proposing in a few months. He didn't want to rush things too much, but he already knew that he wanted to marry her. He loved her deeply, and it was getting more difficult to be apart from her.

He shook his head to clear his thoughts and turned his attention back to the computer screen. It wasn't like him to daydream at work. He worked through his break because he felt guilty for taking work time to think about Maggie. By the end of the day he was caught up and felt good about himself. He was feeling more confident in every area of his life, and it felt wonderful.

Kate's mother got to her house in record time and she was at the emergency room within an hour. She was still having some mild cramping, but it hadn't gotten any worse. After an endless stream of forms and questions, Kate was escorted back to a room, where she waited a long time before the doctor finally came to see her. He was an older man, probably in his sixties, Kate decided, with a balding head, and kind eyes. He introduced himself as Dr. Graham.

After a brief exam, he explained that he wanted to do an ultrasound to make sure the baby was okay. He tried to reassure her that many women have spotting during their pregnancy, and that they were still able to carry the baby to term. The fact that she was well into her second trimester was a good sign, he said.

He must have noticed her wedding ring, because he asked if she would like for him to try and reach her husband. Maybe it was from the stressful day, or the fact that she was worried sick that she might lose the baby, but suddenly she found herself sobbing as she told Dr. Graham about the events of the day. He listened quietly, and then patted her hand. "Just because you and your husband can't see eye to eye does not change the fact that he is the baby's father. My guess is that he would very much like to know that you are here and what you are going through." With that he turned and left the room.

Kate watched the ultrasound technician as she carefully moved the wand back and forth over her abdomen. She was looking at her face hoping for a reaction, but the woman was void of emotion as she concentrated on the screen.

Back in the room, Dr. Graham finally came in with a smile on his face. "I've got good news!" He came and sat next to Kate. "The ultrasound shows that your baby boy is just fine."

"Baby boy?" Kate's eyes went wide.

"Oh I am so sorry! You didn't know the sex of your baby?"

Kate smiled. "I wanted to know, but my husband didn't. Now that it appears I am on my own, I am glad you told me."

Dr. Graham told Kate she needed to take it easy for the next week or two and try and stay off her feet as much as possible. If the bleeding or cramping became worse, she needed to call her doctor or return to the hospital. Other than that, there really wasn't anything more she could do. Kate thanked Dr. Graham for everything. She was still considering what he said about Matt as she left the hospital. *Maybe I'll call him tomorrow,* she thought.

Chapter Twenty-Seven

Gina packed the last of her things in a huge suitcase. She was excited, scared, and sad all at the same time. Saying goodbye to Vivian would be the hardest of all. She just kept thinking of Damian and the hope of things to come. Damian was so excited he had called her already to see if she was on her way. He had offered to fly to New Mexico and drive out to California with her, but she refused. She wanted the time to herself to be alone with her thoughts. It was a big step leaving the Blue Moon and taking a chance on love. She was not one to follow her heart easily, and at times she wondered if she really was doing the right thing. But all it took was hearing Damian's voice, and her doubts faded.

Her aunt and uncle had returned the week before and seemed to have things running smoothly. They were impressed with all she had done at the Inn while they were traveling and were very grateful that she had given them the opportunity to see the country. But they were glad to be home now and wished Gina the best in her new adventure.

Gina was nervous about starting a new job but excited to be doing something she thought she would love. She was also scared about giving her heart to Damian. But she knew in her soul it was too late. She was in love with him, and she would just have to deal with the fact that his job was being a United States Marine. Her parents were ecstatic that she was moving back to California and were looking forward to meeting Damian.

As she put the last of her things in the trunk of her car, she went to say goodbye to Vivian. She found her out on the patio watering the flowers.

"I'm all packed and ready to go." Gina sat down on the glider.

"I've decided I'm not going to say goodbye. I'm just going to say see you later, because I have a feeling you'll be back," she said as she sat down next to Gina. They glided in silence for a few minutes.

"I'll miss you, you know, and your family." She tried unsuccessfully to hold back the tears.

"I'll miss you too." Vivian wiped the tears from her eyes. They stood and gave each other a long hug. They promised to call each other and email. Vivian was staying on at the Inn to help her aunt and uncle, and she was grateful to keep her job.

After saying good-bye to her aunt and uncle and Oliver, Gina headed out to the interstate. She cried for the first few miles, but after that she began to look forward to the future and not dwell on what she was leaving behind. She knew it was time for her to go. It wouldn't have been the same trying to run the Inn with her aunt and uncle there.

She called Damian's cell and left a message that she was on her way. She knew he would be checking his messages on his lunch break and would call her then if he could. He had rented an apartment for her not far from her new job. He was amazed that she trusted him that much, but was immensely pleased that she did. It was a small one bedroom apartment, with a nice outdoor area. It was bright and sunny, and the moment he saw it he thought it suited her. He hoped she liked it. He had insisted on paying for the deposit and first month's rent for her, despite her protests. They were going furniture shopping when she got there which she thought would be interesting. She hoped his tastes would be similar to hers.

The drive to San Diego was beautiful. The mountains looked majestic with the sun shining on their jagged peaks. The sky was a brilliant blue, and there were only a few small clouds in the sky. Damian had called her on his lunch break. He was so excited that she was coming he had a hard time concentrating at work. He told her he had a surprise for her when she arrived. He was going to meet her at her apartment and promised they were going to celebrate. "Only after you help me unpack the car," she teased.

When Gina pulled up in front of the apartment complex, she smiled from ear to ear. She only hoped she liked the inside as well as the outside. It was a quaint two story building painted a sunny yellow with white trim. There were flower boxes on the windows, and she noticed there were flowers already planted in all of them. It was on a side street with not much traffic and the smell of eucalyptus filled the air. She stepped out of her car and found herself in Damian's arms. He still had his uniform on, and he looked so handsome it took her breath away.

When she stood back and looked at him, she laughed. "I don't know if I should kiss you or salute you."

Damian took her by the hand. "Kiss me, definitely." He kissed her passionately before he led her into the entry way and opened the door to her apartment. Gina looked around in amazement. Damian had furnished her entire apartment, down to the pictures on the wall. She was speechless. The style and colors were exactly what she would have chosen herself. She was overwhelmed by his thoughtfulness.

Damian stood back while Gina walked around the entire apartment. She opened doors and cabinets and looked at every detail. Finally she came back into the living room, with a huge smile on her face and her eyes wet with tears. "I love every detail." She threw her arms around him and hugged him.

"That's good, I was getting a little worried when you were taking so long looking at everything." Damian grinned, as he kissed the tip of her nose.

"How did you know what I would like? It is exactly what I would have chosen myself."

Gina sat down on the cream-colored couch. It was so comfortable and was lined with bright pillows that matched the chairs in the room.

"I paid attention to details at the Inn, plus a little intuition. I wasn't sure you would like everything, so I made sure we could return anything you didn't like." Damian sat down beside her and took her hand. "I didn't want you to have to worry about furniture and starting a new job all at the same time. Besides you only have a few days before your new job starts, and I wanted you all to myself." Gina turned to look at him.

"Thank you so much. You have to let me pay you back for the furniture, that had to be kind of expensive," Gina said seriously.

"No way! You came all the way out here just to be with me, it was the least I could do. Besides I plan on being her a lot, so I'll be using the furniture too." Damian got up and went into the kitchen. Gina followed and noticed something smelled delicious.

"I hope you're hungry. I know it won't be as good as what you would make, but it should be edible." Damian turned his attention to the spaghetti sauce on the stove.

"It smells wonderful. I'm starving because I didn't stop for lunch. I was in such a hurry to get here; I didn't want to waste any time," Gina admitted with a grin. "This has to be one of the nicest, most thoughtful things anyone has ever done for me. I don't know how to begin to thank you." Gina turned as she took some plates out of the cupboard.

"I'm sure you will think of something."

He took the French bread out of the oven and began slicing it. He was already thinking about the diamond ring he planned to give Gina when the time was right. He had picked it out already and had it on hold at the jewelry store. He wanted her to meet his father first. It was the only family he had now, and it was important to him that they like each other. He hoped that Gina would go with him to meet Dave in Palm Springs on Saturday. He was going to propose over dinner. Palm Springs was very nice and would be a shorter drive for Damian. Twentynine Palms was almost a hardship post because the town was remote and small, so Dave had made reservations for them at an upscale restaurant overlooking the mountains in Palm Springs. It was only an hour's drive for Dave, so it worked well for both of them.

They had a wonderful meal together, laughing and talking as if they had been together for years. Gina agreed to dinner with his father and was already trying to decide what to wear for the occasion. After dinner Gina helped Damian clean up the dishes. Next they went to get Gina's things out of her car. Damian was such a gentleman. He refused to let her carry anything that weighed over twenty pounds. They put her things away, and she was amazed she still had plenty of storage space in her apartment.

Damian took Gina in his arms and kissed her. There was such a hunger yet tenderness in his kiss; it almost made her cry. She felt like she was home when she was with him and knew that she was already very much in love with him. She just hadn't wanted to admit it to herself until now. She had found what her heart had been yearning for right in Damian's arms.

The next two days Gina spent getting settled and finding her way around. She had found the post office, grocery store, and where her new job was located. She was glad that it was a short commute for her to work because she hadn't acclimated to all of the traffic yet.

She drove to the base to have lunch with Damian and was pleased that it wasn't difficult to find. She had found a dress shop a few blocks from her apartment when she was out for her morning run. She decided to see if she could find something nice to wear to dinner on Saturday night. She was more than a little nervous about meeting Damian's father. He was a colonel in the Marine Corps after all, and that alone was intimidating. She really hoped he would like her. They were planning on having brunch with her family on Sunday, so by the time she started her new job, they would have met each other's family. She prayed it would all go well.

She found a cute sun dress in a dark-green color that accented her eyes. It had a small shawl that went over it, which she thought would be perfect for evening. She bought a new pair of heels and hoped that the new outfit would somehow give her confidence. At least at work she would be wearing a uniform so that wasn't going to be difficult to dress for each day.

Damian was a little nervous about meeting Gina's family but tried not to let it show. When he picked her up on Saturday he was wearing navy pants and a light blue polo shirt. He looked very handsome. He whistled when he saw Gina in her new dress and heels, which made her blush. It was one of the things he loved about her. She was so beautiful, but yet she didn't make a fuss about her looks.

The drive to Palm Springs was pleasant, and they were at the restaurant before they knew it. They went inside, and Dave was already waiting there for them. He hugged Damian and then turned and hugged Gina. She was surprised at how warm and friendly he was and how he made her feel at ease immediately. They had a wonderful Mexican dinner out on the patio, and she found that Dave was one of the most intelligent men she had ever met. He had been all over the world and yet he remained a man with simple needs and wants. They talked of his travels and of world affairs. Gina was surprised when she looked at the clock and two hours had passed.

Dave excused himself, and winked at Damian. When they were alone at the table, Damian got on one knee and took Gina's hand. She began to laugh and cry at the same time.

"Gina, you are the woman that I love and cherish. I want to spend my life with you. I can't promise it will always be easy, but I can promise that I will love you until

I die. Will you marry me and make me the happiest man alive?" He slipped the delicate ring onto her finger.

"Yes!" Gina threw her arms around Damian, as people at the restaurant clapped and cheered. Dave had been watching from the corner of the room, and was smiling as he made his way back to their table.

Finally Dave paid the check even though Damian offered, and they were back outside. They thanked him for dinner and hugged him. "You are a very lucky man, son." Dave patted Damian on the back. "I think she is a keeper, if I do say so myself." Gina blushed at the compliment. She was the one who felt lucky. Dave whispered in Gina's ear as he kissed her cheek, "If he doesn't marry you, I will." Gina laughed out loud, and hugged him again.

On the way back to San Diego they talked about the evening. Gina told Damian how much she liked his father. She was relieved that he liked her too. They talked about having brunch with her family the next day, and Damian admitted how nervous he was. Gina tried to reassure him, but she understood. She had been nervous about meeting his father as well. Damian was going to pick her up in the morning and then head to her parent's house. They lived about an hour away, and he didn't think traffic would be bad since it was a Sunday. Gina kept looking at the exquisite diamond ring on her finger. She felt like everything in the world was right, even if for just this moment in time.

When they arrived at her parent's house the next day, Damian grew quiet. He kept wondering what he would do if they didn't approve of him. He was in love with Gina and knew he didn't want to spend the rest of his life without her. He only hoped her parents could see that.

Gina squeezed his hand as she led him up the steps. Her parents had a ranch style house with brick on the front. It looked very cozy and warm from the outside, and Damian was surprised at how large it felt once inside. It was decorated in creams and shades of green and looked very elegant. It was a different style from Gina's, but it was nice too. Gina introduced him to her parents, and they went out on the patio to wait for brunch. Gina's mother asked her to help in the kitchen leaving Damian alone with her father.

Her father had a deep tan and a warm smile. He pulled out a flask and poured some rum from it into their orange juice. "Don't tell on me, but this makes these things a lot more fun," he said with a grin. Damian laughed and was grateful. They talked about baseball and the Marine Corps, and soon the ladies joined them. Her father noticed the diamond ring on Gina's hand first, and then her mother began to squeal with delight. They were so excited that Gina and Damian were engaged. Her father proposed a toast.

They had a delightful brunch, and Damian could see where Gina had gotten her love of cooking. The food was delicious, and her parents were warm and charming people. By the time they left, Damian was feeling much more at ease. Gina told Damian that she could tell her parents liked him very much, and her mother had commented to her in the kitchen that she thought he was handsome. Damian smiled that smile that still melted Gina's heart.

Chapter Twenty-Eight

Kate was busy at the flower shop and trying her best to distract herself with work. Her belly was getting quite large now, and the baby was moving around all the time. She was getting a little more tired toward the end of the day, and her feet would swell if she didn't remember to sit down. She had a doctor's appointment that afternoon, and Matt was going with her, despite her protests. She had taken the doctor's advice and stayed off her feet for a couple of weeks, and she had not had any more spotting. She was grateful for Helen and Jody who worked extra hours at the shop during that time.

Matt had moved out, but was being civil. She was trying her best for the baby's sake, but was struggling. She lay awake at night feeling guilty that her baby would be born into an already broken home. Maybe it was for the best, she decided. She blamed herself for driving Matt away. Things had changed between them somewhere along the way; she had just been fooling herself that things would work out in the end. She cried herself to sleep more often than not, but took comfort in the fact that she was not going to be all alone. She reminded herself that many women were single parents and they managed just fine. Matt still wouldn't talk about baby names. Kate had given up on getting him to help with the nursery and had asked her mother to help. They had decorated it in pale oranges, blues, and yellows, and she thought it looked wonderful.

At the doctor's office, they listened to the baby's heartbeat. The doctor told them that the baby was now mature enough that if it were to be born it would survive. Kate looked at Matt and saw relief wash over his face. After they left the doctor's office, Matt turned down a side street and headed to a nearby bistro. "I know you want to get back to work, but I'd like to take you to lunch first." Kate started to protest, but somehow her anger had been replaced by sadness.

They sat at an outside table, and the warmth of the sun felt good to both of them. After they ordered Matt reached across the table and took Kate's hands in his.

"Let's talk about names for our baby," Matt said with a grin.

"Why the change of heart?" Kate said curiously. Matt took a deep breath.

"I didn't want to pick out names or decorate the nursery or do anything that had to do with the baby until I was sure it was going to be a reality. I knew if something happened to this baby that you would be devastated. I wasn't sure I could stand to watch you go through another disappointment. Matt's expression grew serious as he continued to hold Kate's hands. Kate wanted to say something, but she sensed somehow he wasn't finished, so she kept quiet.

"I know all of this has been a shock and I don't blame you if you hate me. I just want you to know that just because it didn't work out for us as a couple, that doesn't mean I am going to run out on our child. I would like to have joint custody and if you think you could find it in your heart; I would like to be there when the baby is born." Matt looked at Kate hopefully for what seemed like an eternity.

Finally, Kate replied, "I know you will be a good father. I only wish we could have been a traditional family to this baby. As for being there for the birth, I will have to give that some thought." Kate fought back tears, as they seemed to come so freely these days.

"Fair enough." Matt had a somber look as he signaled for the waiter to bring the check. They had discussed names for the baby and had agreed on two names for a boy or a girl. Kate kept the fact that she knew the sex of the baby to herself.

"Good news at the doctor?" Helen asked as she put the finishing touches on a spring bouquet.

"Yes. The baby is developed enough now that if it were born it would be able to survive on its own." Kate sat her bag down and put on her work apron. "Then Matt took me to lunch, and we discussed names for the baby. We at least have it narrowed down now," Kate smiled.

"That is wonderful news! I'm so happy for you and for Matt. You two are going to make wonderful parents, I just know it," Helen beamed. Kate sincerely hoped so. She had waited so long for this baby, she was determined to enjoy every minute

She was considering letting Matt be in the delivery room. She had asked her mom, but knew that she would understand if she decided to let Matt be there instead. Her parents had been very supportive, and she knew she could count on them to help her once the baby arrived.

Chapter Twenty-Nine

Frank reached over and kissed Maggie on the cheek. She turned and propped herself up on one elbow to see what time it was. The sun was streaming through the skylight above them, and the sky was a glorious blue. She put her head back on the pillow, as Frank reached for her under the covers. "How is my beautiful wife?" He asked as his hand wandered to her thigh.

"Fabulous," Maggie grinned. Frank turned her toward him and kissed her slowly and passionately. He knew he would never grow tired of this.

He could not be happier. Maggie had become his wife three months ago and every day felt like they were on their honeymoon. Elizabeth had welcomed him into the family, albeit with a little trepidation.

Maggie had sold her house and so had Frank, and they had bought a house together. They decided they needed a fresh start. Maggie was enjoying decorating their home, and she had even taken on a new writing assignment. They had spent hours looking at antique furniture and had chosen some very nice pieces. Elizabeth still had her room at their new house, and she seemed genuinely pleased about that. She and Frank got along well, and she enjoyed coming home from college to see them.

Frank's hand began to caress Maggie's thigh as he kissed her passionately. Maggie groaned. "If you don't stop that, we will be late to the wedding," she teased. She loved being married to Frank and was happier than she had been in a long time. She felt peaceful and loved and was looking forward to their future together.

Out on the patio, Kate was hurrying around arranging flowers and bows. She was so happy to be doing what she loved as baby Seth slept nearby. Matt had come with her to help watch the baby while she decorated for the wedding. They both were crazy about him. He was four months old now, and they adored him. Kate took him to work for a few hours every day, which made nursing much easier. Matt had rearranged his work schedule, so he had the baby in the late afternoons. Seth was a delightful baby and was sleeping through the night now. All in all things were working out. Kate had begun to see her therapist again, and was feeling stronger emotionally. Her parents and friends had been a huge source of strength and support. She enjoyed her job and loved being a mother. In the end, she had decided to let Matt be there for the birth. She was touched when she saw him crying unashamedly the first time he held his son. Kate looked up at the window where she knew the bride was getting ready. She wanted the flowers and decorations to be perfect. They were having a small intimate wedding out on the patio, with a reception to follow. The weather was perfect. Kate placed the last of the orchids near the front of the patio and looked around. Everything seemed to be in order. She went inside to change for the ceremony.

An hour later, the guests were seated and the music signaled that the bride was ready to come down the aisle. Everyone stood and turned toward the bride. The dress she wore was simple but elegant, with tiny pearls accenting her waist. Gina's hand shook as she held her father's arm and looked ahead at Damian and his father. His father was his best man, and the two of them looked stunning in their dress blue uniforms. Vivian was waiting on the other side, looking beautiful. Her dress was the palest hint of yellow, and she held a bouquet of orchids, which was Gina's favorite flower.

Damian stood beaming at her. He thought she was the most beautiful thing he had ever seen. He wished his mother could have seen this day, but he was thankful to have his father by his side. His friend, Greg had come to the wedding and Damian was touched. He stood tall and proud as he waited for Gina to reach him.

Her father kissed her on the cheek and wiped a tear from his eye as he gave her hand to Damian. After that everything else faded away as Gina vowed her love and her life to Damian. She always knew that the Blue Moon Inn was an enchanted, magical sort of place; she just never realized that any of it was meant for her.

Epilogue

Gina sat on the beach watching her beautiful children make sand castles. Zane David had just turned two, and he squealed with delight when the water rushed over his tiny feet washing the sand from beneath them. Lydia was four, and she was very intent on making her sand castle one fit for a princess.

She couldn't believe how blessed she felt. As she watched the sailboats moving over the waves, she thought of how life could hold such treasures. One never knew what might be just up ahead.

Damian had received a promotion in the Marine Corps, and now she was able to stay home with the children full time. His deployments were never easy, but she was grateful to have her parents and Damian's father nearby. The colonel had officially retired and was a doting grandfather when he wasn't busy volunteering as a mentor to ROTC students at the local high school.

Gina had gotten a card from Frank and Maggie along with a picture of them and Elizabeth on a recent trip to Australia. All of them were smiling ear to ear. Maggie had sent her a copy of the novel she had written that was now on *The New York Times* best sellers list, and Gina couldn't wait to read it.

Kate had come by for a visit when she was in town last month. She was looking to expand the flower shop to a second location now that Seth was in school. She and Matt were both enjoying being parents, and she was trying to come to terms with the fact that Matt had remarried. She said work was a good distraction for her now.

As for Vivian, she was now the proud owner of the Blue Moon Inn. Gina's aunt and uncle had officially retired and moved to Florida and sold the Inn to Vivian. She was dating a new guy, one she met while he was staying at the Blue Moon Inn.

Gina smiled as she thought about it. She had that funny feeling that something wonderful was going to happen...again.